F

CUMMINS

Fingala, Maid of Rathay

LARGE PRINT   £8.50

L 5/9

FINGALA, MAID OF RATHAY

On his deathbed, Sir James Montgomery of Rathay asks his daughter, Fingala, to swear that she will not honour her marriage contract until her brother Patrick, the new heir, returns from serving the King. Patrick must marry. Rathay must not be left without a mistress. But Patrick has fallen in love with the Lady Catherine Gordon whom the King, James IV, has given in marriage to the young man who claims to be Richard of York, one of the princes in the Tower.

Books by Mary Cummins
in the Linford Romance Library:

CARRIAGE FOR TWO

MARY CUMMINS

FINGALA, MAID OF RATHAY

Complete and Unabridged

LINFORD
Leicester

First published in Great Britain in 1983 by
Robert Hale Limited
London

First Linford Edition
published 1999
by arrangement with
Robert Hale Limited
London

British Library CIP Data

Cummins, Mary
    Fingala, maid of Rathay.—Large print ed.—
Linford romance library
    1. Love stories
    2. Large type books
    I. Title
    823.9′14 [F]

    ISBN 0–7089–5467–7

Published by
F. A. Thorpe (Publishing) Ltd.
Anstey, Leicestershire

Set by Words & Graphics Ltd.
Anstey, Leicestershire
Printed and bound in Great Britain by
T. J. International Ltd., Padstow, Cornwall

This book is printed on acid-free paper

1

Sir James Montgomery of Rathay moved feebly and indicated that he desired a goblet of water.

All morning Fingala had watched for the arrival of her brother, fearful that their father would die before he arrived, but there was no cloud of dust on the distant horizon, and she feared that the messenger she had sent to Edinburgh with an urgent summons for Patrick to return to Rathay without delay had either been set upon by thieves or had been unable to find Patrick at the King's Court.

Beside the bed her mother, the Lady Agnes, whispered her prayers and counted her beads for the soul of her husband. His health had never been good since he had stood in battle beside his King, James III, and had been wounded in his service. He had

1

been loyal to James when some of the other nobles, with the young fifteen-year-old Prince James in their midst, marched against him at Sauchieburn and tried to depose James and put his son on the throne. Even with the sword of Robert the Bruce in his hands, James III had proved no soldier and he had lost the battle, his kingdom and his life.

Sir James Montgomery had limped home to Rathay, and although he recovered from his wounds his great strength had gone. He also faced a divided household in that he never forgave his new king for riding against his father amidst those enemies. But his own son, Patrick, had been the same age as the new king, and he had thought that no blame should have been attached to the boy.

'Would *you* ride out with your father's enemies?' James Montgomery demanded.

'He had no choice, Father,' Patrick shouted. 'He would have been killed had he not ridden with Angus and Bothwell.'

'They were traitors to their king. They always believed James would have his revenge on them because they killed his favourites. He gave his son into the keeping of Shaw at Stirling Castle, but the insurgents bribed Shaw and took the prince. He rode with them against his father.'

'He has paid for it, even though he was not to blame,' said Patrick hotly. 'Do you not know, Father, that the king wears an iron belt, constantly, under his clothing in remorse for the fact that he rode with the men who killed his father? Every year he adds another ounce of weight to the belt so that his penance should not be relaxed. And he has never punished the nobles who rode at his father's side. Rather he has been generous with nobles on both sides, and has not my mother used the monies paid to us to benefit Rathay? Is it not a more noble castle than it has ever been?'

'Money his father had saved. He will bankrupt our country.' Sir James stared at his son sourly.

'Money his father hoarded,' Patrick defended. 'He was a miser. In fact, it was his love of money which drove many nobles against him and was his undoing.'

'He was the king, and they murdered him,' Sir James stated flatly.

He was aware that he and his wife and family lived a great deal more graciously at Rathay, their large estate near the Firth of Clyde, than his father or grandfather had done. He had been against his wife, the Lady Agnes, spending money on rich hangings and floor coverings, but it seemed to Sir James that times were changing in the country, and that the ladies were being allowed more freedom than was good for them. They were inclined to dictate the affairs of their household where once a baron's word was Law.

As soon as he was old enough to gain his spurs, Patrick had declared his intention of serving the king, and already the sickness which was now ending his life was afflicting Sir James. He might have had other plans for the boy, had he been in the full vigour of his health, but as it was, he sighed and warned Patrick that he must return to Rathay at frequent intervals to help keep the affairs of the estate running smoothly. The nobles were less quarrelsome after they succeeded in murdering King James III, no doubt having exhausted themselves in their struggles to overthrow the king, and fearful of those barons who were not on their side. There had been peace at Rathay for a year or two, though it seemed to Fingala that the younger noblemen often risked life and limb in some of the games they played for the amusement of their king with tilts, tournaments and sword fights, sometimes involving a lady's pleasure.

Fingala would dearly have loved to be a lady amongst the rest, watching even the fiercest of the games with shining eyes, but although she did not always obey her father's wishes to the letter, she could not force his permission to accompany Patrick to court, especially when Patrick had no desire for her company.

'We cannot *both* leave Rathay at the same time,' he argued. 'Our mother is a delicate woman.'

'Our mother is as delicate as steel,' Fingala returned. 'It is our father who ails. Cannot you see the white hairs on his head and the lines about his mouth? The wound in his chest will not heal and is very ill-looking at times. I have to gather herbs to soothe the pain of it.'

'All the more reason for you to stay at Rathay,' said Patrick with triumph. He enjoyed life in Edinburgh, and did not want to be hampered by a woman even if she were his well-loved sister.

'You have secrets in Edinburgh,' Fingala accused him, and Patrick's face suffused with colour. 'It is a lady. I thought it was so.'

'She is — she is fair beyond any woman I have ever seen,' said Patrick.

'So — ' Fingala eyed him gravely — 'fair even beyond your sister?'

'A man does not dwell on the beauty of his sister. I will allow Buchanan to sing thy praises, Sister.'

Fingala's long eyelashes fringed her sparkling blue eyes. She was promised to Sir Kenneth Buchanan of Cardowan, and the match was much to her liking.

'Who is this astonishing Beauty?' she asked.

'I would keep my own counsel.'

'Then she is far beyond your reach? A true goddess?'

'Not so.' Patrick was stung. He knew it would not be easy to win the lady, but he considered himself the equal of any in the land.

'Who?' Fingala repeated.

'The Lady Catherine Gordon, Huntly's daughter.'

Fingala drew in her breath. 'You lift your eyes high, Brother. She is kin to the king and has the reputation of being the most beautiful woman in the Realm. Is it so?'

'It is so,' said Patrick. 'She has also smiled kindly on me and I intend to ask the king for permission to woo the lady. Rathay is a fine property, and if I serve James as well as our father served *his* father, then he could well reward me further and add to our property. It would then be a fine enough property to offer Lady Catherine. Rathay Castle is richly furnished and offers every comfort to ourselves and our guests. I will not be shy about offering for her, Fingala. I hope you will be happy to love her as a sister.'

'And our parents to love her as a daughter? Our father desires that you should marry soon. He would like to see heirs born to Rathay. If there must be delays whilst you try to persuade the king that you are the best possible husband for the Lady Catherine, or if she keeps you dangling whilst she ponders the matter, our father will wish thee to set thine eyes on lesser beauty.'

'I will have no other,' said Patrick, swiftly. 'She is all I desire. If I am refused Lady Catherine, I will have no other female to wife.'

'That is foolish talk.'

'I love her,' said Patrick swiftly, and Fingala softened. In truth she had been caught in the toils of love herself, since she found Sir Kenneth a very handsome man.

Patrick was looking at her hesitantly and a little awkwardly.

'I have heard that some women have strange powers to control and guide the emotions of Love. They have much wisdom with herbs which can turn the heart towards one who loves dearly enough for two.'

Fingala stared at him narrowly.

'I hope I do not understand you, Brother,' she said, 'but it seems you could be speaking about witchcraft.'

He flushed and looked sullen.

'Some say that you have the gift, Sister. None can deny that your herbs can bring the near dead back to life.

Our great-grandmother, who was also named Fingala, was recognised as a witch. Have her powers died with her, or could it be that they begin to live in you?'

'If our father were not losing his health I would make you repeat these allegations before him,' said Fingala, hotly. 'I will not listen to such talk.'

'Do not lose your temper,' Patrick said, placatingly. 'I was making fun, but I can tell you, Fingala, that I would ask the help of a witch if I thought it would gain me Lady Catherine.'

'Then she will be fortunate if she says nay,' retorted Fingala, 'because she would be marrying an ass. Are you going to tell our father about this — this great love of yours?'

'No! Not yet,' Patrick added, less explosively, 'and I hope you will not break my confidence. I will see the King as soon as the opportunity arises for me to serve him, and ask that the matter be considered. If the king is favourable, there will be time to tell our father.'

'I hope so,' said Fingala. 'Do not stay away too long, Patrick. I tell you, he is a sick man.'

'I will be home as soon as I can, Patrick promised, 'but I think you are anxious for nothing. I think our father is stronger than you think.'

'I wish you were in the right of it,' said Fingala. 'If I *were* that witch, as you suspect me to be, then maybe I could save him. But even I cannot go against the Will of God.'

★ ★ ★

Patrick had gone back to Edinburgh, and Sir James Montgomery had spent his days administering his estate with the help of Fingala. The Lady Agnes had ordered new gowns and wore a freshly-starched head-dress every day. She was as bright as a bird, and Sir James preferred her to attend to the lighter things of life. She could sing in a sweet pretty voice, accompanying herself on the lute, and had insisted that Fingala, also, should learn how to play the instrument. But Fingala's voice was rarely heard raised in song, yet when she did sing her voice soared like a bird and the servants would pause to listen, then avoid each other's eyes. It was rumoured amongst them that Fingala, Maid of Rathay, was a witch and could charm the animals and force them to do her will. Even as a child, had she not kept an out-house near the stables where injured animals were miraculously cured of their ills, and would ever more come to her bidding and eat out of her hand? She was too fair for this world, and her voice made the hairs of men rise upon their necks as though they were listening to music from another world.

Also, she worked like a man beside her father, and gave judgements amongst the farmers and labourers which were too wise and well thought out for a woman of her age. She took power upon herself, and it was plain to all that Sir James was beginning to lose his. He had a cough which racked his body and he was forced to take to his bed.

Fingala grew anxious and sent a couple of servants with a message for Sir Patrick, bidding him to return and to receive his father's blessing.

Lady Agnes would not believe her husband was so ill that he might not recover.

'It is only a mild chill,' she opined. 'Sir James must have warmed honey and olive oil. It will relieve his chest. I will sing to him to cheer him up.'

But when she saw that James was in no state to listen to her music, Lady Agnes felt as though a great hollow had appeared round her heart and all her gaiety drained away. Fingala was correct. James was very ill. James looked at her with fever-bright eyes and called her 'Hannah', which had been his sister's name, a sister long since dead.

She went to their private chapel and said prayers for the recovery of her lord, but as he grew weaker she knelt by his bedside and murmured her prayers between shedding her tears. Fingala watched from the window for Patrick to arrive, though her hopes also leaned in another direction. She was promised to Sir Kenneth Buchanan who also served the king and who had been sent on an errand to France. He had taken leave of Fingala with a promise to return as soon as was possible, and for marriage plans to be discussed. Cardowan estate bordered Rathay, and although the Montgomeries and the Buchanans had not always been the closest of friends there had been peace between the two clans since the days of James III.

If only Kenneth would come! thought Fingala, then the days would not seem so bleak.

The weather grew warm, the days were bright and beautiful, and for a short time it seemed that Sir James was a little better, then one evening he called Fingala to his bedside, and she knelt beside him, knowing that death was now upon his face.

'Patrick has not come,' he whispered.

'No, Father, but he should arrive very soon.'

'It is already too late.'

She made no reply, and Lady Agnes wept quietly at the other side of the bed.

'Promise me that you will not leave Rathay until Patrick returns and lives here with a wife to found a family.'

Fingala's heart raced, then cold sickness gripped her. She was losing her father and her grief was very deep, but only the thought of a future life as the wife of Sir Kenneth Buchanan was making the loss bearable for her. Now her father was asking her to give him a promise that she would not marry before Patrick, and Patrick loved Lady Catherine Gordon. Suppose — suppose the king did not consent to the marriage between Patrick and Lady Catherine.

Sir James had grasped her hand.

'You know the estate and how to administer it better than Patrick. I am concerned that Rathay should not be neglected. Patrick will not settle down until he marries. Promise me — promise me, Fingala.'

'Give him your promise,' Lady Agnes cried, her voice hoarse with her tears. 'He is your father.'

Fingala's mouth felt dry. Every instinct told her to give no such promise, but she knew that she had no alternative.

'I — I promise, Father,' she said, and Sir James sighed gently, then relaxed on his pillows.

He slept. In the early hours of the following morning he died.

2

It was worse than anything Fingala could have imagined. They all thought that she was a strong, level-headed woman; the serving men and women, the henchmen, the tenants, farmers and labourers. Even her mother, who should have known better, thought her capable of taking on any responsibility. The mantle of authority had dropped on to Fingala's shoulders and she felt that it fitted her ill.

She had to arrange with the priest to bury Sir James with his ancestors, and she had to take charge of Rathay, even taking over the reins as mistress of the old castle from her mother whose only wish appeared to be a desire to shut herself away and go into unrelieved mourning for her husband.

'My life is over,' she told Fingala.

'It is not over until God decides

for you,' her daughter said, a trifle impatiently. She had not sought such responsibility. If only Patrick would come home and tell her that he was arranging a marriage with some sensible young female, how happy she would be. She would be free to marry Kenneth whenever he rode in to claim her for his bride. As things stood she could never leave Rathay, and as the days began to pass and she became more competent at dealing with the affairs of the estate, Fingala knew that she would not wish to leave Rathay until Patrick could take care of it. She loved it. She had not realised how much she loved Rathay until her father had given it into her hands.

Experience came with time, and the young, rather imperious woman with a face of such beauty that people called her a witch, even though her hair was as bright as ripe corn, began to take control of the estate. The power in her glance could cause strong, powerful men to back away when they would have been aggressive over a land dispute, and her people began to refer to her as the Maid of Rathay. Fingala listened and had no objection to the title.

* * *

Sir Kenneth Buchanan of Cardowan was a fine, handsome man of twenty-six years. He had served his king mainly in France, and although he was pleased with the match his father, Sir Andrew Buchanan, had arranged for him with the Lady Fingala of Rathay, Kenneth had spent his time in France willingly enough.

England and France were once again under the strain of thin-veiled hostility which could quickly be ignited into full-scale war over the disputed territory of the Duchy of Brittany.

But Scotland was not concerned in these hostilities, and James IV had a liking and respect for France born of an allied relationship which had been established over many years. Many young Scottish noblemen liked to offer their swords to France for a number of years. It improved their education and widened their knowledge of political affairs.

There had been other affairs, also, which had attracted Sir Kenneth, and it pleased him how well such affairs could be conducted, with grace and dignity, by young French women who had a practical approach to life, and to love. He had lost his heart several times, but it had always been handed back to him in good condition.

At fifty-three, Sir Andrew Buchanan was growing old, and he decided that it was time to recall Kenneth because he was needed at Cardowan. It was time the young nobleman was brought home and the marriage contract with the Lady Fingala fulfilled. Sir Andrew wanted to see his grandchildren before he grew senile and could not recognise them as his own flesh and blood.

At first Kenneth was loth to part with

his enjoyment of the French court, then something in the remembrance of his own country, cold and bleak though it was after the delights of Paris, tugged at his heart-strings. He remembered the fair wraith of a girl who waited for him, and life began to beckon with its own excitement. The king was a fine sportsman. There would be tournaments in Edinburgh and perhaps even fine sport if he were bidden to ride with the king when he went hawking. And there would be Fingala. The match had been arranged, but he was well enough pleased with the choice. She was a fair enough young maid.

Sir Kenneth returned home as the snowdrops began to fade and the brightness of the daffodils and primroses brought warmth and colour to the country-side. There was great feasting at Cardowan, and two days later one of the henchmen rushed to find Fingala where she was consulting with her factor, John Cuthbert, in the great hall. He was an old man in his sixties, but he had served the Montgomeries as far back as the times of Fingala's grandfather.

'There are horsemen riding in, Mistress,' the man told her, 'and the pennant is that of Cardowan. I think Sir Kenneth returns from France.'

Fingala had spent the morning in the great hall, collecting rents from the farmers and tenants, and hearing grievances. The factor had also informed her that disease had broken out amongst the cattle and that several beasts were already lost.

'The farmers ask the Maid of Rathay to pray for the lifting of such a scourge,' John Cuthbert petitioned.

'The good of Rathay is ever in my prayers,' said Fingala, coolly.

'Aye, but — '

John Cuthbert hesitated. It was difficult to petition the Maid of Rathay without allowing her to find out that the more ignorant of the land-workers believed their animals had been afflicted by an Evil Eye, and that only the stronger powers such as the Maid might possess could fight off this evil. John Cuthbert was disquieted. Belief that the Lady Fingala was a witch was becoming more widespread, and he did not care for such rumours. To him she was still the child of her father grown into the full beauty of young womanhood. Once a reputation for witchcraft was established, it was difficult to dispute. One could only let it be known that the Maid prayed for the good of God's creatures and not for anything harmful or evil. Hence the petition for the removal of the Scourge.

'It gives comfort if you let it be known that you pray for the removal of such evil,' he entreated.

'Very well, John Cuthbert, I will do so,' she nodded. 'I will pray for the scourge to be lifted.'

★ ★ ★

She was tired when the news was brought to her that Sir Kenneth was riding in. Her mother had withdrawn herself into her own chamber after the death of Sir James, and no news had yet been received from Patrick. Perhaps he did not yet know that he was now Sir Patrick Montgomery, Master of Rathay.

Fingala had found the days long and tedious for a young girl, but now, suddenly, the sun shone once more in her heart and the light of happiness and excitement shone in her face so that John Cuthbert surreptitiously crossed himself before her. She had a strange beauty which made her look like no ordinary maid. Perhaps the rumours were not far from correct. Perhaps she had gained the sort of power which some women received. Perhaps the mark of it was upon her forehead.

'We will leave all other business until the morrow, John Cuthbert,' she said. 'I will leave you now. My gown is old and soiled. It would not be at all suitable for receiving Sir Kenneth Buchanan. Send Jane Dow to me.'

'Aye, Mistress Fingala.'

John Cuthbert took his leave, and Fingala flew up the stone stairs, her light feet bare of boots, until she reached her bed-chamber. Minutes later the old nursemaid, Jane Dow, wheezed her way into the room, and Fingala ordered water to be brought so that she could wash the sweats from her body.

'It is not yet warm enough,' Jane Dow grumbled. 'The wind can still blaw cauld and you leave yourself open to illness and fevers.'

'Not I,' said Fingala, joyously, 'I do not ail.'

'It would be better if you did, Mistress Fingala,' Jane Dow said, darkly, but Fingala was too excited to query what she meant.

'There is little time, Jane,' she said. 'Hurry, hurry! We will hear the clatter of the horses in the courtyard at any time. Go! Now!'

Sir Kenneth had thought his future bride a comely enough young woman, but now he saw that he had been mistaken. She was beautiful beyond belief. He strode into the great hall, demanding to see the mistress of the household in order that he could pay his respects, but it was Fingala herself who stepped forward to greet him so that he was halted in his tracks.

'My mother is secluded in prayers for my dear father,' she explained. 'His death has grieved her beyond measure. I take care of our affairs in the absence of my brother who serves the king in Edinburgh. You are welcome to Rathay, Sir Kenneth.'

His face had lit up with delight at the sight of her, and he could see that there would not be quibble about honouring their betrothal. She wore the heavy betrothal ring, set with garnets and river pearls, which had been formally handed to the Montgomeries by Sir

Andrew Buchanan when the contract was made.

'There is none to see me claim my bride then, little White Heart?' asked Sir Kenneth. 'But I do so, and with a willing heart.'

He had come forward to kiss her hand, and his eyes devoured her proud young figure and glowed with delight at the beauty of her face.

'By God, but you have grown into a fine woman, Fingala.'

'I am glad I please you, Sir Kenneth,' she said, smiling.

'There is none to see if I claim more than a polite kiss on the hand. I need to remove my travel-stained garments, but I cannot wait to kiss your lips.'

She was clasped against his chest while he kissed her soundly, then with reddened cheeks and some laughter she pushed him away.

'I had thought your manners would be more exquisite after the French court,' she protested.

'Ay — the French court! I am a

native of my own land. We like to live like men, as God made us.'

He was removing his garments, and Fingala ordered food to be served, also to Sir Kenneth's squire and henchmen.

'It would appear you have travelled from Paris, and not Cardowan,' she commented.

'We had some sport on the way,' he told her. 'I am happy to be home.'

'But so desirous of renewing acquaintance with your bride that you spend the day hawking.'

'I had no notion of the pleasure that awaited me at Rathay.'

He looked well-formed and handsome of face as he stood before her clad in finest linen and velvet, cut in the French style. Her heart beat almost to suffocation with excitement, but she was in command of herself once more. There was no man likely more to please her than Sir Kenneth, but she was not a woman who would put herself completely into a man's power.

'I had come to claim you, now, as

my bride, Fingala, but I find myself at a loss, unless your mother consents to see me ere I go. I would take thee with me, back to Cardowan, if the priest will marry us in your chapel on thy mother's consent.'

'She is not well, Sir Kenneth. My father's death was a great blow, as it was to all of us. My brother has not been home since. There are messengers sent out thrice to find him, but always he has moved with the king and the messengers cannot find him, or are too lazy to try. The last one was lazy and needed his hindquarters warmed. The one who took his place will surely be more successful. Until then, I can do nothing.'

He frowned. 'Do nothing? What do you mean, that you can do nothing?'

She prevaricated as the food arrived, and Sir Kenneth fell upon it hungrily. His sport had given him a prime appetite. His knife had been well cleaned and glinted as he ate his food, and he drank his wine from a silver goblet which he quickly replenished.

'Since there is none to say us nay, I think we can forget the priest for tonight,' he decided. 'I would fain get to know thee better, Fingala. I think we would pleasure each other for many an hour.'

Fingala's face grew rosy. She had not a doubt of it, but her code of conduct was greater than that. She wanted the blessing of the priest upon their union in case they made a child together who would not find favour with God because his creation had not been blessed.

'Not without my consent,' she told him, 'and I do not give it.'

His eyes narrowed. 'What is this? Are you not a generous woman?'

'I would like to think I am generous, but my favours will never be given lightly, even to you.'

'The ladies of the French court were not so backward.'

'I have heard their skirts are light. I doubt if they will remember thee for long, Sir Kenneth, but even now be employed in giving their favours elsewhere.'

'By God, their tongues are more gentle even if their bodies are warm,' he said, his eyes glinting.

'Do not expect a meek and mild nature from me, Sir Kenneth,' said Fingala, proudly. 'We women have had to keep the castle fires burning too long while our menfolk go to war. The properties, so furiously fought over, would have been poor estates but for the women who helped to administer them in the absence of their lords. I will not be a subserviant wife to thee, if you claim me as a bride. You had best ponder that matter, Sir Kenneth.'

Her head was thrown back proudly, and the anger began to fade from his face.

'Why do we quarrel over things of such small importance?' he asked. 'We waste time, Fingala. I am hot for thee.'

'And I am circumspect, even though

31

I wear the betrothal ring. I would have the priest bless our union, and I cannot do so, as yet. I am pledged to Rathay until my brother returns.'

Sir Kenneth had drunk a third goblet of wine, and now he pushed the remains of his food away. He turned to look closely at Fingala. She was not proving as easy as he had supposed. He had thought to claim her as his woman without any delay and to dispense with a great deal of formality since Sir James had so recently died, but she was not so ready to fall into his arms, and he began to feel anger and resentment.

'What is this?' he asked, suspiciously.

'What I say.'

Fingala's face had grown white. When she had made her pledge to her father, a coldness had come upon her heart and she had known that trouble might come of it in the future.

'Do I take your meaning that you will not honour our pledge until your brother returns?'

'Aye, and with a wife,' said Fingala,

bravely, 'with a woman who will take over as mistress of Rathay and breed children so that our line will be continued, and Rathay made safe. My father was dying. He asked for my pledge, that I would keep the castle safe for my brother. My mother is sick. She has lost her strength after my father's death, and he could see how it would be for her — '

'Wait!' commanded Sir Kenneth.

The wine was beginning to sit sour to his stomach.

'Have you not yet commanded your brother to return? And what of a woman for him? Did not Sir James arrange a match even as he made sure of our own? What kind of nonsense are you telling me?'

Fingala paled at his tone. She could see the controlled fury in Sir Kenneth, but she knew that his wine had fumed into his head. Some men could become unreasonable with wine when they were normally of a merry nature. Sir Kenneth was surely one of these. A short time ago he had been full of cheerful spirits and longing to join with her in pleasure that their future lives would be bound up with each other.

Now he looked at her with a stranger's eyes, and her own anger stirred. Surely he could understand her position. Was it so strange that she should promise her father to secure Rathay before she became wife to Sir Kenneth? He was showing a selfish streak if he refused to understand, and she bit her lip. It was no doubt born of impatience for her, nevertheless she would have to be wary of this if they were to live happily together in the future.

But she would never be meek and mild as a wife for any man. Sir Kenneth had better know this before they were wed, so she continued to regard him steadily.

'My brother has already given his heart to a woman,' she said. 'He loves the Lady Catherine Gordon and will have no other.'

Sir Kenneth stared at her, then his eyes beamed with derision and he began to laugh.

'Now I know you have lost your wits, lady, even as your brother has lost his. Half the men in Scotland could say the same. Do half our nobles go celibate because the daughter of the Earl of Huntly can only marry one man? And that chosen by the king! What makes Sir Patrick Montgomery so special that he thinks the king will give him the fairest woman in the land? The Montgomeries are not of royal blood. They are not the greatest in the land.'

'We are an old and honoured family,' cried Fingala, hotly. 'Why should we not be as good as any? If the Lady Catherine desires my brother, why should she not have him?'

'Aye — if! She can have the pick of the country.'

'I am surprised that you do not go and offer for her yourself!' cried Fingala, goaded.

His eyes narrowed. It was the first bit of feeling she had shown towards him, and the hint of jealously pleased him.

'Perhaps she is only the fairest because few have seen thee, Fingala, Maid of Rathay,' he said, slowly. 'Why cannot we forget your stupid brother? I will help thee to keep a firm hand on Rathay until he returns. We are wasting time. We can send for the priest and make our vows tomorrow, or the next day. For now, let us have time to ourselves, Fingala. I need thee, White Heart, I need thee.'

Her heart melted and she was suddenly warm with love for him, but the spectre of her father's face rose before her and she could feel the hot dry hands which had clutched at her own, and hear her own voice making the promises, promises on a death-bed.

'Do not ask it for tonight,' she said, painfully. 'I must find my brother and hand Rathay to him. If — if he is dead — God forbid! — then that is a different matter. We would then have to make ourselves responsible for Rathay.'

'That *would* be a different tale,' cried Sir Kenneth. 'Why should I dangle at thy skirts waiting for thee? You have broken your pledge, my dear Fingala, to *me* by keeping faith with thy father. Do you think about that? I am a proud man. I will not be a laughing-stock while you ponder on whether to be my wife or your brother's keeper! I ride out again, and if, one month from this day, you have not come to me and have left Rathay behind and all responsibilities for your brother's miserable estate, then our contract is at an end. I am a fair man. I cannot deal with thee more fairly. Do you not agree?'

Her heart was paining her. She longed to tell him to ride out and forget her, but she had been pledged to Sir Kenneth for a long time and she had known that her future lay in Cardowan. She was no longer a very young maid and she did not wish to live and die without savouring the full flavour of womanhood. Besides, in spite of his belligerence, he was a handsome man.

But — one month? It was no time to give her, even if Patrick could be found. It would take longer than a month to establish him at Rathay.

'Three months,' she amended.

Sir Kenneth's eyes smouldered. Three months! Why should he wait for three days, since he wanted a wife now? She was an arrogant young woman.

He turned to look at her, ready to repudiate the contract now, but his tongue seemed to cleave to his mouth, and he saw her as a bright flame which seemed to grow in power and beauty even as he stood in front of her. He tried to speak, but could not, then his tongue was loosened once more.

'Three months,' he agreed.

'It is fair,' she said, quietly. 'I will come to you within three months or — or not at all.'

'I will not be made to look a fool,' he told her in a low voice which trembled a little. This girl had power over him, power to make him do her will, and power to reach out to him in passion. His fatigue was great.

'Rouse your man and see that my servants are made ready to ride out. We do not spend a night under the hospitality of Rathay.'

They rode out an hour later, and the Rathay servants cast surreptitious glances at the Maid and crept about with still tongues and sideways glances. Some made the sign of the Cross. She had kept her anger in check until after Sir Kenneth had gone, but now it blazed from her eyes.

She snapped out orders for the security of the castle, and they were obeyed immediately.

3

News was coming out of Edinburgh that the king entertained a stranger claiming to be the young Duke of York whom everyone believed to have been murdered in the Tower of London. Sir Thomas Gilfillan, friend to Sir Patrick, had ridden in to Rathay on his way back to Edinburgh, together with his young brother, his squire, and several henchmen. He had brought news of all that was happening at Court.

'The king is enchanted with the man who is a plausible fellow,' said Sir Thomas, easing out his long bulk on a wooden settle. 'He lookes like a princeling, though none of us have a notion what the young duke looked like, or if he resembles the man the duke would have become, had he lived.'

'The Lady Fingala's head reels,' his young brother laughed, 'and her mother, the Countess of Rathay, has no notion what you talk about, Brother.'

Lady Agnes Montgomery had come downstairs to welcome her guests, but the vague look in her eyes told its own sad tale. She was no longer interested in the outside world, but to Fingala it was of paramount importance. Any news of the king might give a clue to the whereabouts of Patrick. Even Sir Thomas Gilfillan had no news of him.

'Be at ease,' he had said, placatingly. 'there is dissension at Court, and I have no doubt Sir Patrick is one of the prime dissenters. There are those who support the king whether he is right or wrong, and who fawn on him at Court, then a great many of the barons are not so enchanted with our young guest, and think the king is being duped. There is much talk about sending for those who can identify the duke, and who can say with all certainty whether he is York, or whether he is an imposter who is living richly and at his ease in the Scottish Court. James has no love for King Henry. It would suit him very well to put this young Richard on the throne of England because he thinks he could influence him greatly. But some of the older barons can see that the boy is not so simple as he looks. There is a crafty look in his eyes, and we wonder if he is not putting the fool's cap on the head of our king and making our country a laughing-stock.'

'But surely our king is not the man to make himself a laughing-stock,' Fingala protested.

'No, he is a strong man, and brave. Not like his father. But he can also be stubborn when an idea is put before him and he thinks he has the right of it. No, we will have to prove the duke an imposter and allow the king to find the proof for himself before he will withdraw his support from the man. I would not doubt that Patrick is with a few barons of like mind, who are working hard to expose the fellow. He will be too busy to remember Rathay.'

Fingala's lips pressed together. It was time that Patrick remembered Rathay and knew about the change in his fortunes.

'Buchanan of Cardowan has also ridden to Court and supports the king,' said Sir Thomas, jovially, then his eyes narrowed.

'I mean the son — Sir Kenneth — I thocht ye promised to him, Lady Fingala.'

Her face was white, and she nodded slightly but gave no indication that she wished to discuss the matter. Sir Thomas nodded in return. He knew when to hold his tongue and he could sense that all was not well with that marriage contract. He sighed. He had left his own young wife with his mother and was glad to escape from their quarrelling tongues. But she was a sweet, simple child. Fingala of Rathay was beautiful, but she was too much the man for him. Maybe Buchanan was of a similar opinion.

'You are welcome to make a long

visit,' Lady Agnes invited. 'It is good to have a man who is our true friend under our roof.'

Sir Thomas turned to her gently.

'That is well said, lady, but we are bidden the Court, my brother and I. He is about to become squire to Angus.'

'A powerful baron.'

'Powerful indeed. Young James, here, will have to look to himself, as well as his master.'

'Rathay has no master,' said Lady Agnes, sadly, 'only a Maid. They call her the Maid of Rathay, Sir Thomas. She even governs my life.'

'You would wander a-field, my lady mother,' said Fingala, patiently.

'It is quiet here, now that Sir James has gone. An old woman is finished when she loses her man.'

'There is still much to do, Mother,' said Fingala, patiently. 'Have you forgotten that the tapestries must be mended?'

'Everything must be so fine nowadays,'

said Lady Agnes. 'When I was a child we threw rushes on the floor and left the walls bare. We lived well enough. Now we must all be fine to show our foreign guests that we are gentle, cultured people when our men still make the blood flow out of one another. My lord would be alive today had he not fought in battle.'

'They were honourable wounds,' said Sir Thomas uncomfortably. He enjoyed a good skirmish himself when the occasion arose, and proudly displayed one or two healed wounds.

'I beg leave to withdraw,' said Lady Agnes. 'Fingala will entertain you, sirs.'

Fingala escorted her mother up to her chamber.

Two days later Sir Patrick Montgomery rode into Rathay accompanied by a band of servants, and two strangers who were to be his guests for some time.

★ ★ ★

All morning Fingala had dealt with petitions and complaints, and her spirits were such that those labourers and small farmers who had merely come to whine over imagined slights and grievances wished they had stayed at their own fireside and put up with the clacking tongues of their wives. Fingala's depression was such as to encourage her to make harsh decisions, and some who came to beg for more found themselves paying a fine instead.

'I think the Maid of Rathay should rest herself,' John Cuthbert said with great dignity. 'You are not yourself, Mistress Fingala. Sir James would not approve of some of the judgements you are making.'

'Someone must make them,' said Fingala, bitterly. 'It must be me, though I like none of it. But I must keep the castle fires a-burning for my brother when I would be away about my own business.'

John Cuthbert eyed her with sympathy.

Every servant at Rathay knew about the storm which had blown up between their lady and Sir Kenneth Buchanan. They had to acknowledge that Sir Kenneth could not be blamed for wanting his contract fulfilled, but they also had sympathy with their lady. She was too good for Sir Kenneth, was John Cuthbert's opinion. But then, opined Jane Dow, who was nursemaid to the Lady Agnes, John Cuthbert would think their lady too good for the king himself. And the Lady Fingala would not be the choice of every man.

Fingala was persuaded to lie down in the afternoon. She had worked night and day since her father died, and had paced the floor waiting her brother's return. Now the strain was being written on her face and in her temper. It was time she rested, thought John Cuthbert.

Fingala consented to lie down for an hour, and all petitoners could be seen on the morrow. She would not admit to her own fatigue, but as she lay on her bed her body throbbed with tiredness, then eased as the rest began to bring new strength to her limbs. She even slept for an hour.

Then suddenly the castle brimmed with life, and Jane Dow came rushing to her with the news.

'Sir Patrick rides in, Mistress Fingala. He has strangers with him. One lies slumped in the saddle and might be ill or wounded. The other is a lady.'

'A lady!'

Fingala's fatigue vanished in seconds. Patrick was coming home with a woman! She could not imagine it would be the Lady Catherine Gordon who was kinswoman to the king himself, but maybe Patrick had come to his senses and had been willing to settle for less.

She pulled on one of her better gowns and took time to fasten a head-dress to her hair, a head-dress which gave her all the dignity due to a lady of the Realm, then she went to inform her mother who was not having one of her better days, before descending to the great hall.

'You must welcome Patrick and his guests, my lady,' she told her mother. 'I will come for you if you do not fell well enough to meet them now.'

'Patrick will come to me,' said Lady Agnes. 'I thank God that he is safe and I am weak with the relief of it. I will welcome the guests later. You can take my place, Fingala.'

The girl sighed. 'I will attend to it, Mother,' she agreed.

★ ★ ★

But when the guests rode in Fingala forgot about all else in attending to the grey-faced man who had to be carried into Rathay. Patrick had welcomed his sister with a warm hug, and she held back from him, noting the strain and fatigue in his eyes. Patrick had been through a bad time.

'I have newly had your message,' he said. 'The messenger said he was the third you have sent to find me. I have been in Fife, then into Cumberland.'

She stared. 'What business had ye in Cumberland, Brother?'

'That I will tell thee,' he promised, 'but the tale will be long in telling, though enough to say that I have been looking for proof to expose an imposter. I have brought two guests, Sir Andrew Heron of Havarden in Yorkshire, and his daughter, Mistress Judith Heron. Sir Andrew has been wounded when he was set upon by thieves and robbers. One of them stuck a sword in his shoulder and it must have been a poor piece of metal because the wound is bad. He has lost much blood.'

Fingala was already giving orders to have Sir Andrew Heron conducted to a guest chamber, then she turned to the young girl who was also dropping with fatigue.

'Mistress Heron. I am very glad to welcome thee to Rathay.' She turned to Patrick. 'Do I welcome the lady as my sister-to-be?' she asked, bluntly, and Patrick coloured deeply.

'I declare you are no more delicate in your tongue than you were as a child,' he declared. 'The king should have bidden you to Court where you might have learned manners.'

'I should have been glad to go to Court,' she reminded him, 'except that my brother would have none of it!'

'That is long since past. I merely give Sir Andrew and his daughter shelter until he is well enough to return to England. I have encountered them in the way of — ah — business.'

'I ask pardon of Miss Judith,' said Fingala, deeply disappointed. The girl was too fatigued to care.

'I am grateful for the hospitality,' she said. 'It would go ill with my father had he met no kindness from Sir Patrick.'

'I will arrange a chamber for you,' said Fingala.

Now that the girl's travelling-cloak had been removed, she could see that she was little more than a child. Yet the child was pretty, with soft dark hair and large pansy-brown eyes. She was too young for Patrick. Ah well, perhaps there was yet another female to take his fancy. Marry he must! She was set on that. Else how could she live her own life? She would lose Sir Kenneth and her chance to be Mistress of Cardowan.

'We will all rest, including my henchmen,' said Patrick. 'So I am too late to bid farewell to my father and to receive his blessing?'

'Aye, you are many days too late, Brother, and you have trapped me at Rathay,' said Fingala, rather sourly. 'I am sorry, though, since your heart must be grieving. Our mother no longer is a strong woman. She is waiting for you in her chamber. Go easy with her, Patrick.'

'I will be gentle. We have much to talk about, Fingala. Did you know that the king has brought that man who calls himself the Duke of York to Edinburgh? He is bending himself towards raising an army to set the man on the English throne.'

'I have heard the rumours,' said Fingala. 'Is he not, then, the young duke?'

'You know very well that the Duke of York perished in the Tower of London. He *and* his brother, God rest them. This man is an imposter.'

Patrick's eyes smouldered, and Fingala looked at him with speculation. Why was Patrick so sure that the man was an imposter? Had he received proof in Cumberland? It seemed to her that Patrick had a lot of explaining to do. And who were these guests of his? Ordinarily he had no love for English people. Perhaps it was no bad thing that he had not brought the girl here as his bride.

Patrick was striding towards the stairs and his private quarters.

'The king marries the Lady Catherine Gordon to York,' he said, 'but I say he marries the finest lady in the land to — to some low-born imposter. I tried to find a man who could identify him in

Cumberland, but he was dead — killed by spies, I have no doubt.'

Fingala caught her breath, and again Patrick turned to look at her and his eyes blazed with anger. And at last she began to understand.

'Oh Patrick,' she said in a low voice. 'You bring ill news if your heart is still given to Lady Catherine.'

'It will never belong to anyone else,' he said, bitterly, 'but she is lost to me now. The knot is already tied and I saw the man's eyes as they rested on her. He will make sure that she belongs to him. It maddens me that she should be ravaged by one such as he, who is not recognised in England — his own country — if his tale be true. Yet they make a laughing-stock of him, as I found out from my journey, *and* of our king for believing his tale and — and supporting him. I tell you, Fingala, it is not to be borne.'

'Go and rest, Patrick,' she said, quietly. 'I am glad you are home.

When you have rested I will hear the whole tale.'

'Look after this guest, Fingala,' he said as he turned away. 'He may yet be the answer to our cause. That imposter has not yet heard the last of me.'

4

Mistress Judith Heron was almost fainting with fatigue and nervous fears. They had been promised a splendid escort, she and her father, if they rode north and accepted the hospitality of the Earl Seton of Kilblain, but as they had ridden through the wilder parts of the Border country the escort had been unable to prevent them being set upon by a band of robbers, and Sir Andrew Heron and his daughter had lost everything they carried.

Sir Andrew had fought bravely, as had the henchmen to Seton, but their squire had been killed and Sir Andrew cut down. Judith had washed and bathed her father's wound, deeply anxious that he should stay alive and that she would not be left orphaned. Ten months ago her mother had died in childbed, the third child born to her since Judith. When Sir Andrew had been approached by an envoy of the Earl Seton of Kilblain, asking him if, for a fine reward of gold, he would ride north and identify the Duke of York as the Prince of England he claimed to be, Sir Andrew had been sorely tempted since the money was needed for his estate.

For a time in his early twenties he had been tutor to the young Princes, and Sir Andrew knew that he would have little trouble in identifying the young duke. It would give him great joy to do so because he had grown fond of the young princes, and the knowledge that they had not, as he had been informed, sickened and died whilst in captivity, gladdened his heart.

Sir Andrew was a scholar as well as a soldier. He was a man of peace, even as he did not hesitate to draw the sword should the need arise to defend himself. The death of his wife, together with the only son born to him, had been a bitter blow and he had wandered aimlessly around Havarden and reflected sadly on the future. He bore an old and honourable name, and although he loved his daughter and would see her married to a man worthy of her, he knew that he would have to make special provision for Havarden. There was no son to inherit the land which had belonged to the Herons for generations.

Sir Andrew had, in the beginning, refused to see the messenger from the Earl of Kilblain, believing the man to be a mad fellow, or one who loved to laugh at the discomfiture of others. What could such a man want with him? Yet the man was a squire and accompanied by two fine servants, and there was an escort of well-disciplined henchmen. The quality of their apparel was also such that gave Sir Andrew pause for thought. Yet why should a Scottish baron wish to consult him? He was no great soldier worthy of the notice of his enemies.

Curiosity overcame his misgivings

and he received Squire William Keith in his business-room and learned that the young man who claimed to be the Duke of York was now the guest of the King of Scotland, James IV. The young squire's task was a delicate one. He had no wish to infer that his king was lacking in common sense, but he reflected the views of most of the Scottish barons who were being asked to form an army in order to restore Duke Richard to the throne of England. James had no love for King Henry. It would pleasure him to have a young king on the throne and one who owed that proud position to himself.

'My master knows that you were tutor to the princes,' said Squire Keith, quietly. 'He has been to Court in Edinburgh, and cannot suffer to see our own king being made to look a fool. He sees a sly look in the man's eyes and extraordinary delight in the way he has been received in Scotland. The king has even offered him the hand of his own kinswoman, the Lady Catherine Gordon, who must surely be the most beautiful woman in our country, and the man swaggers and postures until my master was forced to remove himself from Court or his temper would have put him at odds with his king. Nor is he the only one, sir. There are others who feel the same. There are others who seek true identification of the man, but Earl Seton feels that you are the best man to approach, one who would be trustworthy and know how to hold his tongue. You must have known the young princes well. Even if you do not recognise the man, what child can forget his mentor? Earl Seton would pay well in gold coin if you make the journey, sir.'

Sir Andrew Heron had smiled obliquely.

'A man would require to be well paid to make such a journey,' he remarked. 'A gentleman does not wish to be caught in the crossfire of your warring lords.'

'Our king brings peace and prosperity to our country, said Squire Keith, proudly. 'Many visitors from other countries are guests in my own and do not complain about the hospitality. It is true that we tend to settle our own disputes with all speed, but our nobles prefer to settle their differences in a tournament nowadays. There is plenty of entertainment for the young Duke Richard. You will not be wearied by lack of it.'

'It must be considered carefully,' said Sir Andrew. 'I will make arrangements for you to be my guest, together with your escort, until I have time to ponder the matter. I have buried my wife, but I have a young daughter to consider.'

'My thanks for your hospitality, sir,' Squire Keith bowed, 'but for a brief time only, if you please. The matter is urgent. Even now there may be unrest once more in the country as the king tries to gather an army together. Or perhaps someone else has been found who has sworn to the man. We have a fine escort, too, but I will only be at peace with myself when we ride into Kilblain and I deliver you into the care of the Earl.'

Sir Andrew looked regretfully at his many books and papers. His work would require to be laid aside until this matter was settled.

'Tomorrow,' he promised. 'Tonight we will eat and rest, but I need time to make arrangements for my daughter.'

He picked up the hastily-scrawled invitation written in Earl Seton's own hand. Truly he was not a scholar, but the sum offered was a tempting one. It would provide a fine dowry for Judith when the time came for her to marry.

Judith was still a child who had learned her letters and was still learning the arts of running a household under the tutelage of Sarah Campion, who had been nursemaid and companion to the Lady Eleanor Heron, Judith's mother. It was Sarah Campion who made Sir Andrew's guests comfortable and provided food and wine of which none could complain.

* * *

When Judith knew that she was going to be left at Havarden in the care of Sarah, she rebelled with such noise that Sir Andrew almost refused her a place at the dinner-table.

'I declare that you had best stay in the schoolroom,' he told her. 'I had thought to have a lady at my table to bid my guests welcome.'

'I shall grace your table, sir,' said Judith, proudly.

'You are too young. You have newly proved that to me with your manners and ill-temper.'

'I am fifteen years old, Father. Some females are married at fifteen. Sir, I will grace your table, but you are surely aware that — that to leave me here now that my mother is dead is cruel. I would be alone. Oh sir, Sarah is no companion for me, she is too old. I would ride with you to Scotland.'

Sir Andrew's brows drew together.

'That is not possible. It would be madness to take a child like you on such a journey. You do not understand how hazardous it could prove, besides the many days in the saddle.'

'Then the journey is not fit for you to make,' said Judith, 'if it is fraught with danger. I beg that you do not go, whatever the reward. Cannot you see how ill that goes with me? I cannot sit at home with Sarah Campion, but she could ride with us. She is a strong woman and can make the journey with ease, and care for me as we ride north.'

'Do not plead for something which I do not intend to give,' said her father, brusquely.

He had dressed for dinner in a fine velvet coat, and although his hair had grown silver threads in recent months he was still young and strong. His face was full of noble strength, and Judith feared that he might take a wife before she was settled in marriage to someone she could admire and learn to love. Stepmothers were notoriously jealous of young female children of her age, thought Judith, shrewdly, and she desired to have her own future settled before the memory of her mother receded from her father's heart.

Sir Andrew Heron was a quiet man who did not notice the passing of time unduly. Judith was going to have to fight him for her future. Already she should be promised to a suitable man, but her father only thought her fit for the schoolroom. She did not intend that he should go on a long journey where she could no longer keep him under her eye. He might even bring home a wife from Scotland! Judith's panic increased at the thought and she made a great deal of noise to force his attention. Now she realised that this had been too much, and she grew quiet and dignified, but still determined to have her own way.

But as she sat down with their guests at dinner they paid her the courtesies due to a daughter of their host, then forgot about her. Judith sighed and longed for her sixteenth birthday.

Sir Andrew Heron fought a long hard battle with himself against going to Scotland at the behest of Earl Seton. For the most part, his country was now at peace under Henry VII, even though there was a great deal of civil unrest in the country ever since the Wars of the Roses. Sir Andrew could not but be aware of an underlying Yorkist conspiracy to remove Henry from the throne. The King's right to the crown was based on the weakness of the Beaufort connection, and the Duchess of Burgundy, sister to Edward IV, was almost fanatical in her desire to see Henry Tudor removed from the throne of England.

Sir Andrew's father, Giles Heron, had also been a man of peace though he had worn the white rose. But having been sickened by bloody wars and strife, he had come to accept the ending of the War of the Roses with relief. He had served his king, Edward IV, with loyalty and obedience. He had bent his energies towards educating his son into a much wider knowledge of world affairs, believing that the only way to peace and salvation for one's country lay in education and a desire to promote the beauty of life rather than its ugliness.

Sir Andrew had become a noted scholar and had been called to Court to serve his ailing king. It was then he met Richard, Duke of Gloucester, who took a keen interest in the education of the young princes who were his nephews, and, it seemed to Sir Andrew, directed his considerable energies towards looking after the government of the country on his brother's behalf.

But a dispute over Havarden land, which was being claimed by their powerful neighbour, Knaresborough, had gone against Sir Giles Heron, and

Andrew was given leave to return to Havarden where his father had suffered a stroke. He had gone into the matter of the land claim and began to see that although government was the rule of law, the interpretation of that law was many and divers.

Sir Andrew began to make an extensive study of the law, and his life's work was being devoted to writing a treatise on the justice of manorial stewards and an edition of the statutes.

News of important events in the country often disturbed him at his work. The king died and, later, there came the whispers that the young princes had been murdered in the Tower of London by their uncle, Richard of Gloucester, who had claimed the throne and now ruled as Richard III.

Sir Andrew was distressed. He could not reconcile the image of such a monster with the man he had known, and the fate of the young boys lay heavily on his mind. His wife, Eleanor, tried to influence him into leaving his research work and his writings, believing that he was fast becoming an introspective men, but already her health was becoming affected by pregnancies which ended either in abortion or still-births. Only their oldest child, Judith, survived, and as Sir Andrew grew more absorbed in his work he also grew less involved in political strife.

Entertaining travellers at his table, he could not but be aware of the many factions which continued to writhe like snakes under the apparent calm of the country. When King Henry came to power, Sir Andrew had grieved for Richard, but his mind had quickly grasped the power and sometimes even the devious effects of Henry's government, so that by means of careful planning and, Sir Andrew suspected, bribery, he was bringing his country to peace and prosperity.

Sir Andrew Heron had no wish to see the treacherous days of internal strife returning once more. It did not please him that the Scottish King James was planning to gather an army round him and to march into England to put the young Richard of York — if the young man *were* Richard of York — on the throne. Men would have to fight and give their lives for such a cause, and his own work which he hoped would add to the great law books of England might serve no useful purpose. Men forgot about the law of the land when they went out to fight wars, and to place a new king on the throne.

Yet it would be pleasing to him if the man living under the protection of the King of Scotland were truly the young prince grown up. Sir Andrew had been fond of his young charges. He had grieved for them at the report of their deaths, and it would vindicate King Richard, since he had been blamed for their deaths. He had gained a reputation for being a monster which, Sir Andrew was sure, he did not deserve. Some men said he had poisoned his wife, Anne Neville, so that he could marry his own niece, the Princess Elizabeth, and thereby truly secure the throne. Sir Andrew did not believe it.

He paced the floor of his chamber and debated the point. If he went to Scotland and identified Richard of York as being truly the man he claimed to be, then he would have peace of mind and would have done the memory of King Richard a great service. If, on the other hand, he saw that the man was an imposter, perhaps James IV would abandon his purposed war, and the barons would be relieved of fighting for a cause in which they had no heart.

Yet if the young man *was* Richard, the war would be fought with a vengeance. Men who had catechised King Richard, blaming him for murder, would now be obliged to fight for Richard of York, if only to whiten their souls.

In his ponderings, Sir Andrew took

time to look more closely into his own life, and he did not like what he saw. He had grown soft in his pursuit of knowledge and his determination to bring a true interpretation of the law into all courts. He had grown cowardly. He was still a young man, but his blood had become thin and it was time that he was drawn from his cocoon. A man should live like a man now and again, and not like a monk.

It was time, too, that he paid more attention to the running of his own manor, Havarden, even without the acres which now belonged to Knaresborough. It was time they were made more productive and yielded more income. The money offered by the Earl of Kilblain would be helpful in this venture.

Sir Andrew spent some time in his armoury before he finally rested, but by morning he had his answer for Squire William Keith. He was ready and willing to accompany him to Kilblain where he would accept the hospitality of the Earl Seton, and agree to any arrangements the earl wished to make for positive identification of Richard of York.

★ ★ ★

Sir Andrew refused to allow his daughter to accompany him to Scotland. It was true that the Scots were now more hospitable to their English neighbours, but a fairly long journey to whatever destination was bound to be uncomfortable and more than likely hazardous for a young female.

His temper grew short with his daughter. He had allowed Lady Eleanor to be the greatest influence in her upbringing, except for teaching her her letters, and now Sir Andrew believed this to have been a mistake. She was more than usually wilful for a young female of her age. Then he perceived that there was fear in his daughter's eyes, and that his departure for Scotland had come while the child was still grieving for her mother.

Again he debated with himself. Judith was young and strong. She was well used to sitting a horse and could no doubt spend long hours in the saddle. If she were under his own protection at all times he could not foresee that any harm would come to her. The escort was well armed and well used to the territory through which they must travel.

Sir Andrew made his wishes known that they must carry the minimum of luggage, and that Sarah Campion should accompany her young mistress. Sarah viewed the journey less rosily than Mistress Judith, and would prefer to have remained at Havarden, but she knew her place and that was at the side of Mistress Judith. The Lady Eleanor had given her daughter into Sarah's keeping and that meant being with her at all times.

Squire William Keith could not control his glowering looks, however. Having the care and protection of a young girl would add to his responsibilities and delay their arrival at Kilblain by a great deal of time, a loss of time which might even be dangerous.

But Judith, having won her battle, was equally determined that neither her father nor his escort would be inconvenienced by her, and after Sir Andrew Heron had made his preparations for the safe-guarding of Havarden in his absence, and the party began their long journey, the young girl rode, as Squire William was forced to admit, like a boy.

Unfortunately, however, Nature intervened, and after a few days in the saddle, and nights in wayside inns which were not always clean or comfortable, Judith found herself with a problem which could only be shared by Sarah Campion.

The party was delayed, the result being as Squire William had feared, that as they rode through great lonely stretches of moorland they had to ride for a much longer time in order to reach the shelter of the next inn than originally had been planned. Squire William's eyes were keen and very anxious as he cast about for signs of small bands of thieves who still roamed the wilder territories. His men were also kept on the alert, and Squire William constantly urged Sir Andrew and his daughter to ever greater speed. They became exhausted by their efforts and the henchmen fatigued through lack of sleep.

They did not see their assailants until they were within a reasonable distance of Edinburgh, and Squire William breathed a sigh of relief. He had successfully conducted his party through Border country which was normally beautiful to him, but could be bleak and dangerous if one was bent on a mission.

'We will rest short of Edinburgh, sir,' he advised, 'then turn west towards Kilblain. We bear towards Glasgow and the Clyde and you will be able to rest at Kilblain before proceeding to Edinburgh with Earl Seton. Mistress Judith might be glad to remain at Kilblain,' he added, very formally. She had been a responsibility who might have jeopardised all of their lives.

After another day in the saddle they paused to rest, and Sir Andrew turned to ask Squire Keith a question, but seconds later he was thrown from his horse and was fighting for his life as silent shapes appeared out of the mist.

Squire William grasped Mistress Judith from her mount, also Sarah Campion, and threw the girl into her arms, rushing them towards the shelter of a few trees, then he turned to fight off their assailants. Judith's body, already weakened by the fatigue of the journey and her adjustment into womanhood, refused to obey her mind, when she would have staggered to her feet and tried to help their party. Something buffeted her on the head and she fell to the ground.

When she came to her senses, several

men lay dead or injured, including her father, and their horses and baggage had completely disappeared. Her horror at her situation was such that she could not even scream for help. Sarah Campion also lay beside her with an ugly wound on her forehead. She, too, was dead. Squire William was missing, but as Judith once again fell to the ground with faintness and sickness, then staggered to her feet, she found him lying dead where his body had been thrown amidst a few bushes of hawthorn.

Judith knelt by her father's side. He was still breathing and she murmured a prayer of thanks-giving, even as she also said prayers for the dead. He was bleeding from a wound on his shoulder, and Judith knew that his life was greatly in danger.

It was then that a small party of horsemen rode towards them, travelling towards the west, and Judith staggered to her feet and waved her arms. It no longer mattered that they might be another band of robbers. She had nothing to lose but her life, and her father was rapidly losing his unless something could be done for him.

* * *

It was Sir Patrick Montgomery who found them and who conducted Sir Andrew Heron and his daughter to the shelter of a farmstead whilst he reported the villainy to the local magistrate who would redouble his efforts in administering the law in order to find the thieves and murderers.

'They will be caught, Mistress,' Sir Patrick said. 'My Lord Seton will not rest. Squire Keith was his own nephew and he loved the boy like a son. I knew him well and counted him a friend.'

Judith could only nod. Her shock had been great, driving her into herself so that she seemed to view the world from the imprisonment of her own particular cage. Her father's wound had stopped bleeding, but the old woman who stuffed herbs into it shook her head sadly.

'It was made with a rusty auld blade,' she said. 'I've seen a wound like this afore. Even if the murderers didn't break his head, they poison the body with their nasty weapons.'

Sir Patrick Montgomery had been to Fife to consult with the Earl of Angus, but when he managed to talk to Mistress Judith Heron and to learn the purpose of their journey to Scotland, he became very anxious and protective of Sir Andrew Heron. He paid the cottager well for their care and protection.

'As soon as he is fit to travel, if we can gain him a little strength, I will take you both to Rathay. It is on the Firth of Clyde,' he told Judith, 'but the journey is not too difficult. It is my home. My sister is a fine nurse. She has looked after my father this past few months, and I think she can heal your father, Sir Andrew. I would fain use his services when he is back to his strength again.'

Judith stared at him stolidly. He was a fresh-faced man and solicitous of her, but she had nothing in her which could respond to another human being. Only her father. She looked into his grey face and her heart felt cold with fear in the certainty that one day his laboured breathing would cease.

'You understand? You agree?' Sir Patrick Montgomery insisted. 'I would have him carry out his mission. He will yet receive all payment due to him, but he must not go to Edinburgh until he is well. Permit me to arrange for his removal to Rathay. I will see that the journey there is as comfortable as possible for both of you.'

Again the nightmare of travel began, and Judith could not tell night from day, or how many days she spent in the saddle, or how they rested each night. A strong bearded henchman took care of her father, feeding him small drops of nourishment, even as he insisted that Judith also eat the food which threatened to choke her.

She had grown silent and withdrawn and could find no conversation for Sir Patrick on the journey to his home. She no longer cared where she travelled so long as her father remained alive.

Then one day Sir Patrick Montgomery whooped with joy and informed her that the old grey castle they could see in the distance was Rathay. Judith looked at it with misgiving. It was a cold, bleak-looking place compared with Havarden.

'We are home, Mistress,' Sir Patrick was shouting. 'Your father will be well cared for now.'

'If he still breathes when he is lifted from the saddle,' she muttered. There had been a flush of fever on the man's cheeks for the past two days.

Sir Andrew Heron was still breathing, but it was almost imperceptible.

5

Mistress Judith Heron had never before seen anyone more beautiful than the Maid of Rathay. After her day of terror when those about her whom she had come to know, and those she loved, had been cut down, she had thought that the world was full of ugliness.

Sir Patrick Montgomery had done his best to restore her nervous fears, but he was a Scot and her trust in the Scots had been badly shaken. She had grown up in the peace and tranquillity of a home where her father had revered learning rather than wars and battle, and now every man who drew the sword appeared aggressive to her. Sir Patrick had been gentle with her, and impersonal, treating her like a child who had to be cared for because he needed the services of her father.

When she walked into Rathay, Judith

had been too fatigued to notice that it was anything other than a place of shelter. Then a tall young lady had walked towards her, white-robed and with hair which glistened like spun gold. Her eyes were as blue as aquamarines, and she had looked keenly at Judith as though she were truly interested in her as a person. Judith had wanted to curtsey before her and pay her homage, but instead a bright-faced serving woman had conducted her to a bed-chamber, small but richly furnished, and Judith had been relieved of her soiled travelling clothes, the only possessions left to her, and she lay on sheets of linen which soothed her into sleep.

'My father — ' she had muttered, drowsily.

'The Lady Fingala sees to your father, Mistress.' the woman told her in a strange accent, but pleasing enough to the ear.

'Who — who is the Lady Fingala?' she asked.

'Why — the Maid of Rathay,' she was told.

Judith drifted into sleep, her fears soothed for a short while.

★ ★ ★

Fingala was, indeed, endeavouring to take care of Sir Andrew Heron. He had been put to bed in the sickroom, and Fingala bade Jane Dow help her to attend to the injured man. Each of them drew breath sharply when they saw the extent of his wounds, and Fingala muttered a few unintelligible words over the poultice which she applied to the man's shoulder.

Jane Dow's lips tightened. Sometimes she was at a loss to understand the Maid, and often wondered if she were a changeling child. She had not been present at the birthing of the Lady Fingala, but Jinnet Murdie, who had been midwife and nursemaid to the Lady Agnes, had sickened and died when the child was only a year old, and forward for her age. Already she had been able to totter around on her tiny slender legs, and she addressed everyone by name. She also spoke the unintelligible words of babyhood, but Jinnet had been heard to say that the Lady Fingala could speak properly if she wished and that the words were not the talk of an infant. Then Jinnet grew short in the breath and fell to her death one morning as she climbed the kitchen stairs, and none had been near her at the time.

Jane Dow loved, and feared, the child even as she loved and feared the woman. The Lady Fingala did good deeds for the benefit of poor people, but she would mutter under her breath when she saw the need for it, and human misery aroused her to anger rather than compassion.

But Jane Dow's loyalty was given to Lady Agnes, and her love was for the new master, Sir Patrick. As a little boy he had been given into the keeping of Jane by Sir James

Montgomery, himself, and she loved him more than she would have loved her own child. She had guided his footsteps and had watched the child grow into a man; a fine handsome man equal to any in the land. Jane did not understand why he set such store by this Englishman he had brought to the castle, but she knew that this Sir Andrew Heron was precious to the young master. If the Lady Fingala was chanting incantations, and entreating the Little People to use their powers to put life back into the man's body, then she would stop up her ears and not allow the words to frighten her. Though for Jane Dow, the Little People were capricious and best left alone to their own business.

Fingala, meanwhile, had selected the herbs most likely to draw out the poison of the man's wounds, murmuring the name of each one as she remembered the recipes she had learned from an old cottage woman. With Jane Dow's help, she sponged the dirt of the journey from the man's body, looking down into his bearded face. He was not an old man, as she had supposed, since his daughter was a grown female. Although he was more slender than the men she knew, she could see that his body was well-muscled. He could well be a strong man, though Patrick's lip had curled a little when he talked about him.

'I have found out more about the man,' he said. 'He is to be the guest of Seton, but I knew he would not last the journey to Kilblain and might have poor nursing when he arrived. No matter. I brought him here to Rathay instead of Kilblain. It is in my thoughts that he could do his work equally well from Rathay as Kilblain. I will see Seton and tell him I have his man, and that we will do our best to put him back into the land of the living. We only need him well enough to take a look at the Man in Edinburgh. I will not call him Richard of York! Yet the king would have us fight for him as such.'

'How could he make such a claim if he is not the true prince?' asked Fingala, as she and Patrick had eaten a solitary meal together. 'How would he know how to act the prince if he were an imposter, and low-born, as they say? Surely our own king would recognise that he has no royal blood in his veins.'

'Blood is blood and flows red in the veins in all of us, whatever they say,' said Patrick, spearing a rich piece of meat with his knife. 'He could surely learn his royal manners. It would not be so hard and there are those who would teach him.'

'Who? Who would go to such a pitch?'

'Those who support the Yorkist cause, and the Duchess of Burgundy. She is sister to King Edward IV. She has a great hatred for Henry Tudor and feels he has poor claim to the throne of England. He came to the throne through an illegitimate line, even though it has now been declared legitimate.'

'How so?' asked Fingala, turning her attention to her honey pudding.

'It is the Beaufort line. John o' Gaunt married his mistress, Katherine Swynford, and their children, the Beauforts, were legitimised and given honours, but there are those who still declare them illegitimate, and believe that Henry's claim is weak. If the princes had not died in the Tower, then the claim of the elder, then the younger, would not be disputed. It would be their right of birth. But everyone knows they are dead — murdered — before King Richard took the throne. Now the Yorkists have resurrected King Richard's nephew, one of those children, and have named him Richard of York. Oh, it is clever — very clever — and I can feel it in my bones that the man is playing a part. They can fool our good King James, where they could not fool the English nobles into believing in him. And now James gives him — ' Patrick's voice dropped almost to a whisper — 'gives him the Lady Catherine to wife,' he ended.

Fingala was silent as she considered the matter.

'Does it hurt you so much, Patrick?' she asked. 'Cannot you forget her?'

'Never!' said Patrick vehemently.

'Then what must I do? I gave my promise to our father as he lay on his death-bed that I would stay at Rathay and guard the castle until you returned with a bride who could take my place. But my own marriage contract is now overdue and Sir Kenneth no longer wishes to wait for his wife. I want to live my own life, Patrick, but this — this fixation of yours imprisons me at Rathay. Cannot you see that? What must I do.'

'Restore the scholar to health,' said Sir Patrick. 'He taught the young princes. He says he can identify Richard, but has not said if he has special knowledge which would confirm the man's identity beyond all doubt, or whether it only lies in his eyes, and ears.'

'What of the daughter?'

'The child? She is only a child, but well enough behaved for her years, even if she has nothing to say for herself and makes a dull companion whatever her age. That the scholar should have allowed his child to make the journey to Scotland from his place in Yorkshire shows that he is a man of little sense. We only want his eyes, Fingala, then I will send an escort with him and the girl back to their Yorkshire farms — or estates. He appears to be a man of property. He will be well enough paid for his trouble and that should please him since it would appear that he makes the journey for money, and not from political motives. If you get him well, and soon, then assuredly you can go to Buchanan and we will honour the pledge.'

Fingala sighed. It was not enough. She still needed a female to run Rathay. *Was* the daughter of this man, Heron,

really so young? She needed a young
female, and one had been delivered into
her lap.

Fingala began to speculate, and her
aquamarine eyes grew bright and slowly
changed to green as though the sun had
sparkled on the sea.

6

Slowly Sir Andrew Heron began to recover his senses, though at first awakening he decided that he had perished of his wounds and was now in the next world. An angel stood by his bedside, an angel clad gloriously in white with gold glistening in her hair. She was regarding him intently.

'So our Lord God saw fit to admit his poor humble servant into Heaven,' he remarked, weakly. 'I had expected to roast in Hell for some of my misdeeds, especially in my early years when my brains were few but my desires manifold. Truly He loves the Prodigal Son.'

'He is still out o' his heid,' remarked Jane Dow, crossing herself. 'Poor gentleman. I canna think ill o' him, even though he is English, and they killed my father and brother at Berwick.'

'He is not out of his head,' said Fingala, her eyes still intent. 'The fever has dropped and there is intelligence in his eyes.' She took her patient's thin hand in her own. 'You are still in the land of the living, Sir Andrew Heron,' she said, with a smile.

Pain shot across his shoulder and his face contorted as he moved his body uncomfortably.

'Indeed I am. I would have left this agony behind had I shed this poor worn-out body for one more heavenly. I was misled, Mistress, by the sight of one who looks so like the Angel. May I ask thy name and where I am? I remember nothing of my arrival in this chamber, though I would think that I am the guest of the Earl Seton and I have reached my journey's end. Is my daughter then safe?'

'Your daughter is safe and well,' she told him, sitting down by the side of his bed. 'You were set upon by robbers as you rode for Kilblain which lies two days further north from here. My brother, Sir Patrick Montgomery, found you and brought you here to Rathay to save your life. I am Fingala Montgomery.' 'She is the Lady Fingala, Maid of Rathay,' said Jane Dow, stepping forward to pick up his soiled linen.

'Then I — I think I owe you and — and your brother my life.'

Sir Andrew's voice grew weak and he slumped back upon his pillows.

'He is still very weak,' said Fingala, 'but he no longer faces death. The poisons have cleared out of his blood and his body fights to regain its own strength. My brother will be glad of this.'

Sir Andrew's eyes had grown heavy, and Jane Dow lifted a cup and made him drink.

'His body will rest in sleep,' she said. 'He will be better when he wakes once more.'

'I will go and talk with Mistress Judith,' said Fingala. 'She is with my mother who has developed a fondness for the child. If he wakes again, come for me, Jane Dow. I will be glad to see the man on his feet, and his mission accomplished, then I can begin to live my own life.'

Jane Dow bowed her head. The Lady Fingala's own life would take her away from Rathay. What would the place be like without her hand in it? Perhaps she would accompany her mistress to Cardowan. But would she like Cardowan and the Buchanans? They were a swaggering, lusty family, though their estates much larger than Rathay, and some said their home was very fine and fit to house the highest in the land.

Jane Dow looked into the future and saw changes which she might not like. Sighing, she sat down again on the hard wooden stool beside Sir Andrew Heron's bed and contemplated the Englishman. What would Sir James have said to these affairs? What would he have said to housing an Englishman in his bedchamber? It was time, thought

Jane Dow, that Sir Patrick settled
himself down to looking after Rathay.

★ ★ ★

Judith Heron had been afraid of Rathay,
but as she became familiar with the
well-proportioned rooms, rich hangings
and fine furniture, she grew quiet and
rather shy of her hosts. They were
people of nobility, and she could
only be grateful that the young earl
had rescued her father and herself.
Sir Patrick had appeared to be a
rough-looking man, but having shed
his outer garments and clothed himself
in a fine woollen shirt with velvet coat,
his hair and beard now well-trimmed,
Judith saw that he was a man of
dignity and breeding. He treated her
with polite indulgence, though with an
abstracted air, as one would treat a
child. He even inquired if she wished
to carry on her education, since she
had assured him that her father had
taught her how to write and that she

could read Latin and had translated a manuscript for her father. He thought that the priest might be consulted with regard to teaching her.

'I am no ignorant girl, sir,' she assured Sir Patrick.

'I had not supposed it,' he told her, mildly, 'but I *can* arrange for the priest to continue to teach you in order that your learning might not be neglected, even as he taught my sister and myself.'

'It is no longer necessary,' said Judith, proudly. 'I have grown up now.'

'Do you say so?' Patrick looked at her rounded cheeks and childish form. 'Perhaps, then, you will consent to sit with my mother who needs the companionship of a young lady of culture. She has been unwell since my father died, and prefers to live in seclusion. It is not good for her to cut herself off from other ladies. It encourages her to withdraw into herself and she has no conversation. I am sure that you could rouse her to interest if you told her about your life in England, and how you spend your day. Also she would be interested in your father's work, and your part in helping him.'

'I will be happy to do my best for her,' Judith nodded, gravely, and with all due dignity.

Lady Agnes Montgomery was beginning to neglect her appearance. She had removed her starched headdress, and her greying hair had grown unkempt and required to be brushed and combed by one of the maidservants. But she waved such attention away with a show of impatience. Such niceties were frivolous in view of the greater sorrow she had suffered.

Her face was pale as parchment with her confinement indoors, and Judith eyed her apprehensively. Had she not wished to avoid confirmation of the fact that she *was* merely a child, Judith would have excused herself and run back to her own room. As it was she cast an alarmed look at Sir Patrick as he conducted her into his mother's chamber, then walked forward with his arm round her waist, pushing her forward. Judith stepped to meet the lady, if reluctantly.

'I have brought you a guest, Lady Agnes,' he said, smiling happily.

The older woman looked at him dully, then her eyes turned towards Judith, and she smiled.

'So you have taken a bride at last, Patrick. Your father's soul in Heaven will be content and at peace.'

'Not so,' said Patrick, hurriedly. 'The lady is young, as you see. She is not yet old enough to be a bride. She is the daughter of a guest, Sir Andrew Heron, who has come to serve our country because of his special knowledge. He has estates in Yorkshire, but he is also a scholar and a teacher.'

Lady Agnes' eyes flickered. 'He is English, then?'

'Aye, it is so. He was invited to Scotland by the Earl Seton of Kilblain.'

'He is welcome,' said Lady Agnes

after a pause. 'I would fain meet him, Patrick. Come closer, child, so that I can see you. My eyes are not so young as yours. I cannot see very well where I place the needle, and I use my fingers, but it goes hard with me when I have to look at a new face.'

Judith walked forward slowly, then the light fell on the face of Lady Agnes and she saw the kindness and intelligence in her eyes. There was nothing to fear from this elderly woman.

'That is good, my child. I can see that you are a comely one. Now tell me your name.'

'Judith, Judith Heron, my lady.'

'And you are our guest, also your father. Patrick, my son, I shall sup with you and your guests this night.'

'Sir Andrew is ill, ma'am. He was wounded and robbed. There are brigands yet abroad, though our king has done much to make our country fit to welcome guests. It shames me that Sir Andrew and his daughter have been so ill-treated in our country. But, then, our party had to watch out sharply when we crossed into Cumberland on an errand not so long ago. There are those who obey no laws either in Scotland or England. The priests are lax about doing their work and teaching men how to live in harmony with their neighbours, and reminding them that their souls will roast if they indulge in wrong-doing.'

Lady Agnes' faded eyes held a hint of humour in their depths.

'These are fine words from my son, better than I heard when you went off to fight for your king.'

'I fight when the cause is just,' Patrick muttered.

'Protecting one's country and one's countrymen wherever they are is always a just cause. But this child wants none of the fighting, I am sure. Have you brought her to me, Patrick, because she is idle? I sometimes spend idle hours here, Mistress Judith, yet it is not good to be idle. But I have no strength in my limbs, and my daughter must attend to our affairs. Were I to take charge of Rathay I should forget to tend many of the chores which require to be done to safeguard our home. I am ever forgetful these days. Sit in that chair and you can thread my needle and talk to me. Tell me what is gossip in England. Tell me about Richard of Gloucester. My lord, the Duke of Albany, made friends with him and brought him to Scotland, but the barons did not like him.'

Judith's heart jerked. Patrick had gone, leaving her with this woman who had been so full of intelligence, but whose eyes had not turned opaque and whose voice had taken on a singsong quality.

'He is dead, my lady.'

'He wanted to be king. We have men who desire power in Scotland, too.'

'He was King Richard, my lady. Now he is dead and Henry Tudor — Henry VII is King of England. His queen is Elizabeth, daughter of Edward IV and niece of King Richard.'

'But I know that he was in Edinburgh — or was that a long time ago? I forget, my dear. You see how it is. You are a bright young lady and you can help me to stitch these hangings and fine lace for our table. Your father will be well entertained when he is recovered from his journey. Is he in the sick chambers?'

'It is so, my lady. I thought he would lose his life, but the Lady Fingala has helped him to recover from his wounds. I will be allowed to sit with him soon when he is a little better. I think Lady Fingala was afraid that I would have to watch him die, yet I would have preferred to sit with him even if his life ebbed away. I would want to be with him should — should he be breathing his last.'

'Fingala does not understand?' asked Lady Agnes, her eyes now bright. 'You would stay with your father when he might leave you at any time? You will only be content to sit with me when you know that he is better. Fingala will have sent you away while he was ill, and now she will admit you to the sick-room when he is better. Fingala is not yet full of wisdom and her heart has not yet been touched. She has yet to become a woman.'

The intelligence was back in the faded eyes, and Judith nodded, smiling a little when she saw how well the Lady Agnes understood her own feelings.

'You would do very well for Patrick,' Lady Agnes said, suddenly. 'How old are you, child?'

'Fifteen.'

'Old enough. I may talk to your father when he is well.'

'Oh, no, please do not!' cried Judith. 'I — I believe Sir Patrick has — has other plans.'

Once again Judith felt that Rathay was closing in about her like a prison. Why were the womenfolk so eager for her to marry Sir Patrick Montgomery? He was not attractive to her. She did not want to marry anyone from Scotland, or to be trapped for the rest of her life in this barbarous country, however fine this ancient castle, and however noble her host. She only wanted her father to get well, and for them to return home to Havarden.

★ ★ ★

The Lady Fingala came to tell her that her father was better, and Judith's eyes brightened with hope.

'May I sit by his bedside now, ma'am?' she asked, eagerly.

'For a short while. He is asleep once more,' Fingala told her, kindly.

Judith had tried to insist that she must not be separated from her father, but her plans had been ignored. Fingala had looked at the child, seeing the distress in her soft brown eyes, and the quiver of her young, childish mouth. She had already looked at the man's wounded body and felt that the sickroom was no place for the young girl. The stench of the wound was great until it could be cleaned properly.

Fingala's eyes had met those of Jane Dow and they were of one accord. Gently but firmly she had guided the girl towards Patrick who took her to his mother's quarters, with promises from the Lady Fingala that she would inform them of any change in Sir Andrew's condition. She had then supervised the nursing of Sir Andrew herself.

But now that he was improving, perhaps Judith would speed his recovery. Also, Fingala desired to treat the girl as someone of significance in the household. The young girl's clothing had gone with the robbers, but Fingala had many fine garments, some of which she had outgrown as she attained her full height. The gowns could be made into suitable garments for Mistress Judith, and her long hair could be combed and adorned with a circlet of lace. She could then join Fingala and Sir Patrick for supper in the great hall instead of supping with the Lady Agnes.

Fingala was sure the girl had beauty

and that it could be encouraged to flower under her own skilful handling. And if Patrick had few guests to entertain him, he would be obliged to turn to Mistress Heron. Even a soft word in his ear could draw attention to the fact that the young lady had emerged like a butterfly from its larva, showing her fresh young beauty in bright colours and a new form.

* * *

Judith's heart shook, then warmed, when she saw that her father was, indeed, slowly returning to health. He was sleeping soundly, but the burning fever had left his cheeks and his breathing was regular. She turned to Fingala and decided that she was ready to die for this young woman who had snatched Sir Andrew Heron from the very jaws of death.

'I cannot be too grateful,' she said, humbly and sincerely. 'My father will grow fine and strong again, thanks to you, my lady.'

'He is a servant of God,' said Fingala. 'It is my duty to help him in his need.' She smiled a little. 'And now that you have seen him and are less anxious for his life, Mistress Judith, I would be pleased for you to come with me and we will find you a gown which has not been pulled apart by the brambles.'

Judith flushed. Her travelling-gown was hardly fit to be worn.

'I shall be ever in your debt, ma'am,' she said, ruefully, holding out her torn and bedraggled skirts. 'I had been forced to wear this travelling-gown. It is all I possess.'

'No longer,' said Fingala, happily. 'We will go to my chambers and I will have one of our serving maids bring a selection of gowns.'

'Only one — or perhaps two,' said Judith, 'and I shall return them to you as soon as possible. I hope to return to Havarden as soon as my father can travel.'

'There is no need for such hurry' said Fingala, easily. 'And you must have more than one gown. I have several which are too small, but they could be adjusted for you. You may dispose of them as you wish when — if — you return home. They are no longer of service to me.'

The servant had laid out the gowns on Fingala's bed, and suddenly they were two young females, eager to explore the wonders of finery. Judith exclaimed at the beauty of the stitching, and Fingala assured her that her dressmaker was excellent, and would be sent for without delay. She lived in a cottage near Rathay Castle and stitched to earn coins to help her husband —

' — who is a layabout,' said Fingala. 'I have fined him because he has not tilled his soil and has allowed his property to remain in need of repair after storm damage. But I realised I was also punishing his wife who stitches for his benefit. Be sure that you marry a man who is not lazy, Mistress Judith.

Even a well-born man can be a lazy fellow and not fit to have a wife. My father brought us up to know that nothing can be gained by laziness. My brother has great energy and works to some purpose. He will do well when he takes over the care of Rathay, and his wife will have cause to appreciate her property. My brother will always consider her wishes, I am quite sure. Try this gown, Miss Judith. It is green and should suit you well. I did not care for it, and did not wear it a great deal. It is still very fine.'

It was made of velvet sewn with gold thread, but Judith accepted it reluctantly. Once again she was listening to Lady Fingala singing the praises of her brother.

But the gown suited Judith to perfection, and Fingala almost clapped her hands with delight.

'I knew that it would make you into a Beauty,' she declared. 'See, this lace head-dress goes with the gown.'

She placed it on Judith's dark brown

curls and stood back, her head on one side, then adjusted it carefully.

'You see? It is not of your fashion, but it gives you height and it is very fine.'

It was indeed very fine, thought Judith, much finer than her own clothing. She was torn between delight in wearing something of such quality and reluctance to place herself further in the Lady Fingala's debt. Also there was apprehension that once again she was to be dangled before Sir Patrick. One would have to be a fool, thought Judith, not to realise that the Lady Fingala and her mother needed a bride for the Master of Rathay, and the Lady Fingala wished to hurry the match. It was merely her fate to be available at this time.

'You will wear this to supper in the great hall,' said Fingala, decisively,

'But the Lady Agnes would have me sup with her,' said Judith with reddened cheeks. 'I think she is lonely, ma'am.'

'She will feel better soon, especially — '
Fingala looked speculatively at Judith's
more mature appearance — 'especially
when we have a guest at our table. She
will want to join us for supper. You
are not required to sit with her every
evening or you will encourage her to
take pleasure in her retirement. It is
much more fitting that she should sup
with her family.'

'Yes — yes, I understand,' Judith
agreed.

'You are a young lady of sense,'
said Fingala, approvingly. 'I will send
a servant to bid you to the great hall
when the hour has come.'

Judith had no choice but to agree.

★ ★ ★

Patrick was less easily managed. Fingala
came upon him making preparations to
leave the castle.

'Are you riding out?' she asked, with
keen disappointment.

'Not far,' said Patrick. 'It grows

114

oppressive in Rathay, and John Cuthbert would have me look at two farms who dispute a rented field. Each makes claim to the same field and we cannot find the papers which show the field as belonging to one or the other.'

'Then you will be home for supper?' asked Fingala, eagerly.

His eyes narrowed suspiciously.

'Is it an occasion, Sister? It seems to me that you set store on my presence at the supper-table.'

'It has been quiet, and dull, at Rathay for some weeks,' she said, easily. 'It would give me pleasure not to sup by myself. Our mother lives within herself since our father died. She has not been a companion for me, and I have missed thee, Brother.'

'Is not Sir Kenneth home?'

Her eyes sparkled angrily. 'You know that he does not come because he is offended that I have not honoured our agreement. You know that he waits for me and gives me a short time to fulfil our contract.'

'He is arrogant, Fingala.'

'As I am,' she said, proudly, 'but he is in the right. He would be no man, but a milksop, if he did not show his anger at his treatment. It is for this reason that I am determined that when the first leaf turns golden on the beech-tree, and it drops gently to the grass, then I go to Cardowan. But I must also keep my pledge to our father, Patrick. I must not leave Rathay without a mistress. Since you cannot have the Lady Catherine Gordon, then why cannot you offer for a suitable lady? Mistress Judith is a fine girl and well brought up — '

Patrick rounded on her furiously.

'So I must spend my life in close keeping with a — a stranger's child in order that you can marry Buchanan. Is that what you recommend?'

'She is already leaving childhood behind. She is old enough for child-bearing, and she will not remain a stranger for long.'

'No!' he shouted. 'I will not have it.'

Fingala's cheeks went pink and her eyes flashed green fire, then became bright as aquamarines once again.

'You are a child, Patrick,' she said, evenly. 'You cry for the moon as you did when in your cradle. You are now Master of Rathay yet you take little responsibility for your inheritance. You are happy to bear our name, yet you sigh for the wife of another man.'

'An imposter! He is not who he pretends to be.'

'No matter. He is husband to the Lady Catherine.'

'But suppose I prove him to be someone other than Richard of York. He would lose his head for treason. The king could not object to Lady Catherine marrying again, and this time he might not dally about choosing a husband for his kinswoman.'

'If you are the one to show the king how foolish he is in supporting this man, then he will not wish to reward you.'

Patrick's face flushed. 'You are

always saying I play the idiot, Fingala. You should have been a man. It is little wonder our father has made you châtelaine of the castle. It is a rôle which befits you well. There is little of the gentle lady in you.'

'I am of my race,' she flashed. 'There is little of the gentle lady in any of the daughters of Scotland. It is the women who have been forced to guard the castle while the men rush out and fight one another like dogs.'

'Not so. It is the king who would have his nobles fight for Richard of York. We are commanded to gather our men around us and form an army. If we were the warriors you claim, we would be happy to do so, yet few of the nobles wish to obey the king.'

'Only because you do not like the cause. If King Henry marched north with an army you would polish your weapons with relish and once again Rathay would be guarded by women, children and old men.

'As would Cardowan! Do not forget

that Sir Kenneth will also be gathering his men to the king. He will have no time for wedding thee, Fingala.'

She was silenced. She had not heard from Sir Kenneth since he rode out, but as had always been her way, when she saw a prize slipping away from her she wanted it tenfold. She was fast forgetting Sir Kenneth's ill-temper when he did not get his own way. She could only remember the desire in his eyes when they first rested on her and he appreciated that she had grown into a woman much to his liking.

Fingala's blood had been stirred, and she longed to leave her girlhood behind and face life as a woman, the wife of a nobleman and the mother of his sons. It seemed to her that this young Richard of York stood between her and all she desired, and her eyes once again glittered like aquamarines.

'We must guard Sir Andrew Heron well,' she said, 'and nurse him back to full strength. If he can prove the man an imposter, then let us support him.

Very well, Patrick, raise the money to pay Sir Andrew, or arrange for Seton to pay, and I will have him well for you in — perhaps — a week or two. I will clear the poison from his blood and nourish him so that he regains his strength. And you must be courteous to his daughter even if you do not find her attractive as a woman. She must be happy at Rathay, else she will whine to return to Havarden, and her father will be impatient to take her home. He might then try to hasten his own recovery, and succeed, only, in setting himself further back. Be at the supper-table tonight, and treat the child as a young woman who is owed the courtesies.'

Patrick's sulks cleared a little. For once Fingala talked sense. It was Seton who had sent for Sir Andrew Heron. As soon as he was well he would be taken to Kilblain, and from there he could be taken to Court to identify this Richard.

'I will return in good time,' he

promised. 'It is not true that I have no interest in Rathay. I am going now to see what is required to be done if our farms are to be rich and productive. It is not true that we no longer care for our land, but go warring instead. Our land is precious to us, and the country is fast growing more attractive to guests and to other countries who would trade with us. Our homes are more richly appointed than in the days of our grandfathers, and we are proud to entertain any who would cross our Borders. Let us be rid of this Richard of York and the king will govern well once more. He only supports the man because he has no love for Henry.'

'I am going to the sick-room now,' Fingala nodded. 'I will do all that is required of me.'

7

Sir Andrew Heron's fever had returned in full measure, and he had been muttering and calling for the Lady Eleanor, but when Fingala once again entered the sick-room he grasped her hand and was soothed. His fingers were long and slender, but hot and dry to the touch, and for a while she sat by his bedside, then she released her hand and laid cloths of cool damp linen on his forehead.

'He wants someone called Lady Eleanor,' said Jane Dow.

'His wife,' said Fingala, softly. 'Mistress Judith's mother. She is dead.'

'Poor man,' said Jane Dow, 'and he looks but young. He bears the fine bones of a scholar, and not a warrior. There are no scars on his cheeks, like that cut which Sir Kenneth bears so proudly, and his locks are still plentiful on his head, though some be silver. Yet he must be middle-aged.'

'He is thirty-seven years old. His daughter told me his age when we feared for his life. He is still a sick man, but he will recover. The wound is clean and his fevers grow less. I will feed him hawthorn and capsicum. It will strengthen his heart.'

That evening Sir Andrew woke once more, and this time he was aware of a great emptiness in his stomach and of the need for food. Smiling, Fingala sent Jane Dow to the kitchens for a bowl of nourishing hen broth, but she only allowed him to sup a little.

'I shall feed you again within the hour,' she promised, 'but you must not have too much or your fever will return.'

'So, Fingala, Maid of Rathay, you drive a hard bargain since my stomach now rumbles like an empty drum and I feel the weakness of hunger.'

'Your weakness comes from the fevers,' she said.

'I am more than grateful for my life, Mistress Fingala,' he said, and his dark eyes held hers. 'I know I have been here for a long time — months and months, perhaps — but I have been awake and I know what is owed to you for pulling me from the clutches of the devil himself.'

She was laughing. 'It is only a week or so, not months and months. But my brother, who is the Earl of Rathay, would have you well, Sir Andrew. Do you remember that you set out from England with a mission?'

'I remember,' he agreed. 'It would seem that I have lost the mission. I will also have lost its reward.'

'That you have not. My brother is ready to conduct you to Kilblain when you are better. But you must be strong before you can continue your journey, Sir Andrew.'

His eyes were shrewd as they stared at her, even as he tried to pull himself up in the bed.

'Do not move,' she commanded.

'Jane Dow and I will attend to you for a few days. I cannot risk the wound being harmed.'

'Is it important to you — that I continue with my mission?' he asked. 'Is it important that I identify Richard of York? Do you wish him to be truly Richard, or would you have him an imposter?'

She had flushed. 'It is important to my brother. As for me, I would establish the truth of the matter. My brother has a personal interest. He — he hopes the man is an imposter.'

Sir Andrew regarded her gravely.

'But should the man be truly Richard of York, and I am required to identify him as truly Richard, surely that will be small thanks for your care and attention to me, Maid of Rathay. Will you accept my thanks now, Mistress, before the matter is resolved?'

'I will, and gladly,' she said, and again he grasped her hand.

'Is it yet time for me to eat more of your excellent fare? I declare the first sip only found an empty corner of my stomach. The rest cries out for attention.'

She laughed. 'You have talked too much, Sir Andrew. Remain quiet, and rest yourself. I will find thee some food more to thy liking. I am glad to see thee well. Mistress Judith is a companion for my mother, Lady Agnes Montgomery. She can see you now whenever you wish.'

The dark eyes regarded her brightly again.

'I am glad we are not at war, Lady Fingala. I would have us friends.'

She nodded. She decided that she liked Sir Andrew Heron very much.

★ ★ ★

It was unfortunate that Patrick was not equally appreciative of Mistress Judith, and Fingala thought it a great pity that he had first met the child wearing soiled travelling clothes suited to her years, and could not see that, having

126

now passed her sixteenth birthday and clad in new garments made over from gowns Fingala had outgrown, she was already showing signs of beauty.

'Why do you not take Mistress Judith with you when you ride out to the farms?' Fingala asked Patrick. 'It must be a dull life for a young lady within these walls while we do not entertain. We have had no guests these past three weeks except for packmen and the priest.'

'She should be at her lessons,' he said, sourly, 'and in any case, she does not care to ride with me. She prefers the companionship of our mother.'

'You have asked her?'

Patrick sighed. 'I would remind you, Sister, that this is not the first time you have asked me to entertain Mistress Judith. I have heeded your wishes, hoping to remove the sulks from your face when you look in my direction. I presented my compliments to the child and had arranged for a pony to be made ready for her. Her own mount was stolen by the robbers.'

'She appears to ride well, and I would recommend a better mount. Nor is she such a child. Where are your eyes, Patrick?'

'*Not* resting admiringly on Mistress Judith, I assure you. She *is* only a child. I do not believe she is yet sixteen. I think you mistake the matter, Fingala.'

'I tell you she is sixteen, and you have not issued your invitation in a kindly fashion. She has passed her birthday. I will go now and talk to her, and this time she will be happy to come with you.'

But Mistress Judith's expression became sulky when the Lady Fingala came to find her and ask her to accompany Sir Patrick Montgomery as he rode out to one or two of the farms. John Cuthbert would accompany them, also a serving maid to attend to her needs. She did not like Sir Patrick. She was grateful to him for rescuing her and her father and giving them shelter at Rathay, but he did not trouble to hide the fact that he was bored in her company and found her a great nuisance. He treated her like a young child and almost she had been tempted to act the part, and to play mischievous pranks upon him such as she had played upon her father not so many years ago. A mouse in his bed, perhaps, or the removal of the laces from his shirts. It would be easy to creep into his chamber when he rode out.

But childhood was growing further and further away from her. This journey had made her grow up and she would never be a child again. She admired Fingala, but heartily wished that she would not try to put her into Sir Patrick's company. The more the Lady Fingala encouraged them to be friends, the less they took to each other.

'You need fresh air, Judith,' Fingala told her, firmly. 'It will do you good to have some exercise and ride to Grey Meadow farm. The roof is in need of attention. It caught fire one evening, and but for a heavy downpour the place would have burned to the ground. Now the good wife has to place a bowl upon the floor to catch the water when it rains. Her man will have to be helped into mending his roof. He claims that his back ails him, but John Cuthbert swears that he is as lazy as a dog. Our farmers grew lazy after our father died and now it is good that Patrick should pay him a visit without announcing his arrival, and that he can see what is happening. He depends upon me too much. There is much that a woman cannot do.'

'Then the less people who accompany Sir Patrick, the better,' said Judith, rather pertly, and Fingala frowned.

'I am sure your father would be glad to be out in the fresh air,' she said, pointedly. 'He would be happy to be in your position, and in the full bloom of health, Mistress Judith. It should pleasure you to be able to ride out, if you wish.'

'I ask pardon,' the girl said, humbly. When the Lady Fingala had a certain look in her eye one found oneself agreeing to any suggestion she wished to make.

'I will ride with Sir Patrick,' she said, rather sadly.

★ ★ ★

Patrick's face was like a thundercloud as he rode out of Rathay Castle, accompanied by John Cuthbert, Judith, and one of the maidservants. He motioned John Cuthbert to ride beside him, but the older man held back in deference to Mistress Heron, and with a glint in her eye she spurred her mount and kept pace with Patrick. Her temper was beginning to rise, and the animal, chosen for his placid, rather lazy nature, found himself obliged to move smartly.

The crisp air brought colour to the girl's cheeks, and the apricot velvet of her habit was exceedingly becoming.

Fingala's own maidservant had dressed her hair under her cap, and as she sat her horse, proudly, no one could mistake her for a child.

'I did not beg leave to come with you, sir,' she told Patrick, clearly, 'and if you are going to spend the day in the sulks I shall be happy to change places with the good Cuthbert. The maidservant will make better company.'

He scowled, but the words had jolted him and he turned to look at her.

'The Lady Fingala is too well used to managing my affairs,' he said, stiffly. 'I do not like having my life arranged for me.'

'Nor I,' she agreed, 'and I would have you know that I am not a fool, Sir Patrick. I know she desires a wife for thee and would have me grow to womanhood in front of your eyes. Well, I *have* grown to womanhood, but not to please thee, or the Lady Fingala. It was a natural process, sir. But it need not concern you because my father is not a hard man where his daughter is concerned. Even if you offer for me he would not force me to accept marriage with a man I do not love. And you need have no fear I should ever fall in love with you, Sir Patrick. In fact, I find that it is your conduct which is childish, not mine. You look like a spoiled schoolboy.'

The slow angry colour began to mount Sir Patrick's cheeks. He had had very little conversation with Mistress Judith Heron, believing her opinions to hold little of value to him, and now the child — no, the young female! — was daring to be impertinent to the Earl of Rathay.

'By God, Mistress,' he said, furiously, 'if your father could hear your impertinent tongue he would lay the flat of his sword across your buttocks. In fact, I may do so myself. You are a guest in my house, yet you dare to offer me insults.'

Judith's face had gone very white. She had often been chastised for her ready tongue and had even been soundly beaten when she forgot to keep it under control. Not that it had let her down when it would have been more sensible to stay quiet.

'I ask pardon, sir,' she said, stiffly, 'I — I forgot that — that my father and I owe you, and the Lady Fingala, our very lives.'

'Now you speak the truth!' he retorted, and once again her cheeks flushed at his tone.

She ran a tongue over her lips, then lifted her chin.

'But were it not for your king's desire to fight the cause of the man he believes to be Richard of York, then we would not be travelling in your country and exposed to thieves and robbers.'

Sir Patrick's brows looked thundrous. Did the maid not know when to remain quiet? He had never encountered a young woman so ill-reared.

'I had supposed that your father did not travel here out of charity, and as to thieves and vagabonds, you are indeed fortunate to belong to a country free of such a menace,' he said, quietly, and she flushed rosily.

'It is true,' she agreed. 'A party might be set upon by thieves at any lonely part of a journey in England as in Scotland. I pray my father and I do not encounter any more roving bands as we ride again for Havarden, after he has carried out his duty to you and Earl Seton. The Lady Fingala hopes he will be well enough to leave his bedchamber by one more day, and could be ready for the saddle within one week.'

'He is expected at Kilblain, but you are not,' Patrick said, crushingly. 'It would be safer for you to remain here with my mother. Sir Andrew can ride back to Rathay after he has been to Kilblain and thence to Edinburgh. It is said that the king is preparing to march south with Richard, as soon as a fair-sized army can be gathered together. If the man is Richard, I shall ride out with my own men and join the king with loyalty and obedience. It will then be expedient for you and your father to return to Havarden, but care will have to be taken over planning the route of your journey home.'

'I will not be separated from my father,' said Judith, quickly. 'I made such a noise when he would have left me in Havarden that he was glad to bring me with him to Scotland.'

Sir Patrick smiled. 'And you would have us believe that you are a grown woman! That was the cry of a child who clings to a parent.'

'He is all I have! My mother now lies dead with the other babes who might have been my brothers and sisters.'

'That is no excuse and should not have been accepted by Sir Andrew. I am astonished that a man of his integrity should allow you to ride with him.'

'I would *not* have allowed him to come alone, even with the escort arranged for him. As you can see, I have been rewarded for my foresight. Had I not accompanied my father he would lie dead with Squire Keith.'

Sir Patrick nodded, and there was a hint of admiration in his eyes.

'Perhaps that is so.'

'Then I ride with him to Kilblain and Edinburgh?'

'I have not agreed to that.'

For the first time she smiled, and he was forced to agree with Fingala that the child would be a Beauty one day. But her beauty would not compare with that of the Lady Catherine Gordon — or ought he to think of her as Catherine of York? If the man *was* genuine, then she could well be Queen of England. Already she was beyond his reach.

But not if the man were an imposter, Patrick told himself vehemently. He would die for treason against King Henry, and the Lady Catherine would need a champion. She would not find him wanting. It was unthinkable that she should share the same fate as her husband.

'I think we near the farm you wish to visit, Sir Patrick,' said Judith, urgently, breaking in on his deep thoughts. 'John Cuthbert is giving a signal. See, yonder! I think, too, that you are full of dreams and should wake yourself since you have answered no question for the past few moments. I will say, however, that I am glad the Lady Fingala forced me into riding out with you. The countryside is not as I expected. It is more wild and rugged than my native Havarden, but it is beautiful. I can see distant mountains, and the sea, and the air is pure to breathe. Your acres are very fine, Sir Patrick, and you should do all in thy power to protect them. They are surely a trust given to thee. I will never be a Mistress of Rathay, but I hope you will find such a woman who can warm your heart, and bear you many fine sons for this heritage.'

There was sincerity in her tone, and he softened towards her.

'It is kindly said, Mistress, but I will manage my own affairs and not leave them in the keeping of my sister.

Now we are about our business. John Cuthbert will come with me and we will see if we have a lazy tenant who does not deserve to have the care of his plot, or whether he is a poor sick man who requires care and attention. You will also see what happens to our acres when they are not properly tended and see that it is essential that we have good tenants in our farms.'

'They might have become even more wild and neglected but for the Lady Fingala,' she remarked, then caught her lip, aware that again her tongue had rattled out of her control.

His eyes flickered, and for a moment he looked startled. It was true that he might not have given enough thanks to Fingala for her efforts on his behalf.

'Wait there, along with your maid-servant,' he said, coldly, turning to Judith. 'John Cuthbert, you will come with me,'

★ ★ ★

The farmstead was a poor place compared with others they had passed. The fields looked bare and neglected, and a few emaciated-looking sheep cropped where they could find a few miserable blades of grass. Near the house a plot of land had been dug out in a half-hearted fashion, with rusting farm tools left to lie haphazardly about the place. One or two hens scraped disconsolately near the roughly-hewn door, hoping for scraps which rarely came, and they scattered, squawking, as Sir Patrick accompanied by John Cuthbert strode into the yard. Patrick rapped loudly on the door and listened to the sound of a woman's voice raised in alarm, but no attempt was made to open the door. Pushing it open, Patrick stepped into the dark hovel where a poorly-clad woman was pulling frantically at her husband who lay in a drunken stupor.

'Oh, sir, he — he hasna been weel,' she said, 'sin' the fire. It was a terrible experience for us all, but specially for my man. He's no' been himself at all. It went ill with him.'

'I suspect it's gone ill with him since long before the fire,' said Patrick, heavily. 'His plot has not been dug, nor his sheep driven to new pastures, and we have not yet learned the cause of the fire. I suspect the spirits he is drinking would make a fine blaze, if used in a wrongful fashion.'

The woman went pale.

'It wasna his fault!' she cried, in distress. 'He wasna weel, I tell ye, my lord of Rathay. Ye canna understan' how ill he has been.'

'He has aye been a lazy man,' put in John Cuthbert. 'Where is your water-butt, mistress?'

She indicated the direction in which the water-butt could be found, and John Cuthbert heaved the farmer to his feet, and minutes later the man was bellowing with rage as he was thrown into the barrel of cold water.

Judith moved forward, her eyes wide with curiosity when she saw the spectacle of Adam Johnson being brought to sobriety in order that Patrick could talk to him, and reason with him. John Cuthbert hauled out the man, who was dripping wet, and marched him back into the cottage where he shivered, but eyed Earl Rathay warily.

'Indeed you are a very poor tenant,' said Patrick, looking round the place. 'I cannot have this part of Rathay growing like a weed amongst my acres. I have men a-plenty who would bend their backs to the task of making a fine place of this farm, with good fertile soil and rich pastures for the cattle.'

'Sir, it is as I say,' Jane Johnson pleaded. 'He is a sick man.'

'Then you can pack your bundle and his, and move into the servants' quarters at the castle where a task will be found for you until I find a physician who will tell me if Adam Johnson is at death's door, or if he has merely grown too fond of drinking strong spirits. I will put another tenant into Grey Meadow Farm, but if I find he is in good health then he will be turned off. That I promise you. We have one or two farms in the same state as this, and the estate will be poor unless the farmers are willing to work, and take a pride in their task. The soil is not sour, neither is it full of outcrops. It could be one of the best farms in Rathay, were it to be husbanded properly.'

The man had been muttering sullenly, and now he shook himself like a dog and picked up a rough piece of cloth to wipe his face and hair.

'Give me another chance, sir,' he pleaded, 'and a bit of help with my roof.'

'Ye had that afore!' John Cuthbert growled.

'Aye, but the men only stopped at Grey Meadows for one hour, then left me to do too much on my own. It was hard work for me by myself. If my roof is made safe, I can do my work again.'

'And lie a-bed drinking spirits?' said

Patrick. 'Nay, Adam Johnston, it will not serve. You thought that only the Maid of Rathay would see thy neglect and that my sister would not have my powers.'

'We do not dare to do else other than work hard for the Maid,' said the man, sullenly. 'It is as my wife says. I was ill and took the spirits to get me better, but I am better now. No more will I lie a-bed drinking spirits. I will drink no more. Before God I promise thee, my lord, and I owe thee my allegiance. I have fought for Sir James when I was called to fight, and I will fight for thee, my lord of Rathay.'

Patrick stared at the man. He dared not show weakness or his other tenants would start to grow lax, and the estate would soon suffer and be a poor heritage. In spite of Adam Johnson's protests, it was no doubt because of Fingala's administration that he had allowed his farm to deteriorate without fear of eviction. He would respect her, but he would not credit her with the power to turn him away.

Yet it was not in his nature to allow his tenants to starve, whatever their crime. If he brought the man and his wife to Rathay the other servants would see that they worked their fingers to the bone. There would be no room for laziness in the castle.

'I will ponder the matter until this day week,' he decided. 'The roof will be repaired, but to the benefit of the farm and not merely for thy benefit, Adam Johnson.'

He turned to see Judith standing near the doorway, and when he did not order her away from the place she slowly came forward to stand inside the hovel.

'Gracious heaven,' she said, wrinkling her nose, 'is this the best shelter which can be provided for a human creature? It is no better than that which pigs might expect.'

'It is not the best and it is not the worst,' said Patrick, grimly. 'This is what Adam Johnson and his wife have made of it. Once it was a fine farm and well-maintained, with a farmhouse which was kept clean where a man could be comfortable after a day of toil in the fields. It was a place where children were born and played with contentment, and the smells were from the cooking-pot and not the contents of a jug of spirits. Now it is a poor place, full of dirt and misery, yet the man would have me overlook the neglect and give him another chance. What say you, Mistress Judith? Does he deserve that chance.'

The woman had bobbed a curtsey when she saw the fresh-faced girl. Now she retreated into the shadows.

'If my man does better, then I, too, can do better,' she promised. 'A woman needs a guid man at her back, just as a man needs a guid wife. They should support one another, my lady — my Lord Rathay.'

'Truly said,' Patrick agreed. 'Indeed I will ponder the matter a great deal, but if I decide upon a new tenant you will come to the castle, or take to the road. Do you understand?'

'Aye, my lord, that I do. But I am no beggar, sir, and I have lived and worked at Grey Meadow all my life and my father afore me.'

'And made a poor place of it for your life's work.'

Patrick turned away, heavily depressed. It was what could become of Rathay if he did not take up his inheritance. Yet his heart was empty without the woman he loved and wanted. Could he take another woman into Rathay? This young girl, for instance, whom Fingala dangled before him? But Mistress Judith Heron did not want him any more than he desired her. She was still a mere child to him with her wide eyes and rounded cheeks. He would want a woman who would bear his children.

He kicked at a tree-stump outside the farm-house as he walked towards where the horses had been left tethered, with Judith in his wake, closely followed by John Cuthbert. Life was turning sour for him and, in common with other earls and barons, he wanted this stranger out of his country. He admired his king and thought him misguided to support such a man, yet a great deal of it was rooted in jealously. The man was very handsome and bore the looks and bearing of a prince. If he was not Richard of York, then where had he learned his manners? If he were not Richard of York, then who was he?

And if he were, then Patrick would have to call on his men to ride with him into England and to try to unseat King Henry from the throne of England. Then what would happen to Rathay? Fingala wanted to live her own life, but she had given her sacred oath to their father that she would not leave the place without a mistress. And if Patrick forced her to abide by that oath, it might go ill with her.

Patrick sighed and looked again at Mistress Judith Heron. She was quite in looks, if one could forget Lady Catherine. He sighed again.

'I declare you are like a tired old man, twice the age of my father,' Judith declared. 'You slump in the saddle and sigh with weariness, yet you are not an old man, as I understand.'

'Old! cried Patrick. 'I am twenty-three years old.'

'And I sixteen. Indeed you are old to me. I would have challenged you to a race across the moors, but for the fact that I have been mounted on a lumbering farm animal. He would stop to crop the grass at every turn were it not that I have come to an understanding with him and he knows he had better mind his manners.'

'I gave orders for thine own safety,' Patrick said, huffily. 'It would serve us ill if you were thrown from a spirited mount and have to take your father's place in the sick-bed.'

'My health is more at risk if the beast falls down,' she returned. 'He would be a true friend to the farmer

149

we have just seen. Their steps would match well, one with another.'

'Thy tongue is pert,' said Patrick.

'I am not used to such dullness, whether in animals or slothful people.'

'Then the next time we ride out I will find a dandy fellow for thee to manage.'

Her eyes gleamed. 'Then I look forward to the occasion. I have been spending time thinking up excuses to avoid riding with you again, if you had insisted upon giving me this old nag. But I will do better if you find me a dandy fellow.'

He noticed that her eyes were dancing with laughter and that they were fringed with black lashes. Her cheeks were tinted pink, but they bore the rounded curves of childhood, as did her small chin. What was he thinking about — promising her a spirited mount? He must guard his tongue with the child.

As they neared Rathay Castle they could see that a party of horsemen had ridden into the castle court-yard, and Patrick peered at the pennant.

'It is Buchanan,' he said, 'come to call on Fingala. They are under contract to marry. That should sweeten up my sister's temper.'

'Then there is to be a wedding soon?' asked Judith.

He frowned. 'There has been a postponement. Certain issues must first be resolved.'

'Such as a mistress for Rathay,' said, quietly. 'I *do* have ears, Sir Patrick. I know the position very well with regard to the Lady Fingala. I am sad for her, and sad for thee, sir, but I would have my father and me gone from accepting thy hospitality. I fear we must hinder some of your decisions.'

'A great deal depends upon the health of your father,' said Patrick as they rode into Rathay. 'We can only pray for his good health and the strength to sit a horse once more with the same competence as his daughter.'

He felt angry and at odds with

himself that this girl should show so clearly that he was unattractive to her. She even thought of him as *old*. It piqued his vanity. Who was she, after all, but the daughter of an English gentleman — yes, perhaps nobleman? He pursed his lips. He could not truly complain of her ancestry, always supposing he ever wanted to offer for her. But, of course, such a thing was unthinkable!

She was quite tall, clad as she was in her apricot velvet, and the fresh air had made her skin glow with health, and her eyes were alight with mischief. Her tongue was too merry for a wife! How could he ever have thought her quiet and well-behaved! She would always be forgetful of her manners unless faced with disaster, and she would provoke him to anger very often, even as he felt anger stirring in him now.

Yet he also felt more vital and alive than of late, and his step was firm as they walked into the great hall where Sir Kenneth Buchanan and his squire were being greeted by Lady Fingala and Lady Agnes Montgomery.

'Oh, Patrick, we have a guest,' Fingala was saying, and Patrick noticed that she had managed time enough to change her gown for one which was very grand, and that her looks were exceptionally good.

'So I see,' he said, and went to greet Sir Kenneth. He would have a talk with him later and ask for the latest news of all that was happening in Edinburgh.

'May I present Mistress Judith Heron,' said Fingala, drawing the young maid forward. 'You may have a word with her father, Sir Andrew Heron, presently. He is much stronger today.'

'I had heard that you were entertaining a nobleman from England — and his daughter,' said Kenneth.

He turned to bow to Judith who was staring at him with frank delight. Sir Kenneth's eyes were full of approval as they rested on the girl whose rosy looks made her seem almost like a ripe peach. She, for her part, was enchanted by this tall, broad man clad in the garb of a nobleman of distinction, and one who had learned his manners and gallantry towards gentle ladies at the French court. He had bowed over her hand, and his compliments were expressed in the beauty and flattery of the French language.

'I did not hear that the lady is of such fair beauty,' he said, smiling.

'I am happy to please thee, sir,' said Judith, with all the coquetry of a much older woman.

Looking on, Patrick began to scowl at Fingala whose smile had begun to waver. This was what happened when she encouraged the child to grow up too quickly. Now she fancied herself some sort of enchantress and was trying out her wiles on Buchanan. Well, it would serve her, Fingala, right if Buchanan admired the child openly. She should not have promised their father to put Rathay first. Yet, he thought fairly, how else could she have behaved?

154

Their father was dying. He wanted to die in peace.

That farmer, Adam Johnson, had upset him. He did not believe the man was ill, unless sloth and laziness were illnesses, and he would see to it that the man worked to earn his meat, whether it was in the farm-house or in the castle kitchens.

'How fares Sir Andrew,' he asked his sister.

'Better. His wound is clean and Jane Dow has removed his bandages so that he now wishes to join us for supper in the great hall. I have given orders for special food to be prepared. I do not think it will be long before Sir Andrew is well enough to travel.'

Judith scarcely heard. A day ago she would have been delighted by the prospect of leaving Rathay once more and returning home after the mission was completed. But now life was suddenly blossoming with excitement. She had never seen a more handsome man than Buchanan of Cardowan, and the small scar on his cheek only added to his dashing looks.

She did not care that he was promised to the Lady Fingala, or that he had only ridden in for a short visit. For the moment it was enough to feast her eyes on his great height and breadth. He was splendid, and in her extreme youth she had no thought of hiding her admiration. She would change her travelling-dress for one of the other gowns Fingala had given her. She had not yet worn the cream brocade, and surely it was her favourite!

Excusing herself, Judith hurried up to her bedchamber.

8

Sir Andrew Heron, his wound tightly bound, and well on the way to full recovery, arrived in the great hall in time for supper, and was given a seat of honour at the long table where he could rest his body on the tall back of a beautifully-carved oak chair.

Fingala fussed over him and did not see the sudden hardening of Sir Kenneth Buchanan's eyes, though he was in good spirits and pleased to offer his best courtesy to Sir Andrew.

'I am pleased to have met thee, sir,' Sir Kenneth said, heartily, 'and to know that you may have the means to right what could well be a great wrong. Few of us have a liking for the new friend whom our king has gathered to him.'

'I will do my best to resolve the matter, sir,' said Sir Andrew, smiling at the assembled company, though his face was still pale and drawn with pain. His eyes rested on his daughter, and he tried to hide his surprise that the child should be in such looks. Why, she looked quite grown-up. She was a very different young creature from the child who had thrown tantrums because she was in danger of being left in Havarden whilst he rode into Scotland. Now Judith had acquired dignity and — and a certain beauty, Sir Andrew admitted to himself.

He wondered who, beside the Lady Fingala who had bequeathed the gown, had wrought such a change in his daughter. She had complained that she did not greatly care for Sir Patrick Montgomery, and would prefer that the Lady Fingala should not dangle them in front of each other.

Then it could only be the new guest, Sir Kenneth Buchanan. But he was promised to Lady Fingala. Sir Andrew surveyed Kenneth and Fingala from under his sleepy eyelids. He was a peaceable man and liked to spend his days in peaceful pursuits. It gave one more time to observe one's fellow-men, Sir Andrew reasoned. How would Sir Kenneth react when he found out that he was the object of blatant hero-worship by Judith, because if he knew his daughter, her enthusiasm would overcome her discretion. And there was no doubting that she was an attractive child. And how would Sir Patrick feel when he saw that Judith preferred Sir Kenneth to himself?

Then there was the Lady Fingala. If she saw an attraction growing up between her betrothed and the young maid she had worked so hard to turn into a young woman, would she feel chagrined that she had not allowed Judith to remain adorned as a child? How much would she be hurt if Sir Kenneth's eyes turned to another young woman?

Sir Andrew speculated, then asked himself some searching questions. How would he feel if his daughter was responsible for hurting Fingala in any way? Andrew Heron's mouth tightened. He would not care for it in the least. He was too old for a young lady like the Lady Fingala, but he admired her more than any woman he had known since he lost his wife. In fact, he had fallen in love with her, he admitted to himself honestly. She had nursed him devotedly, and he owed her his life. He had lain on his sick-bed and had watched the sunlight striking through the narrow slats of windows on to her golden hair, and her white gown. She had looked like a creature from the next world, and he, who so admired beauty, had feasted his eyes upon her and had been soothed and rested by her presence.

He looked at Sir Kenneth Buchanan to whom she was promised. What sort of fellow was he? That he was a strong man was there for all to see, but would he care enough about the Maid of Rathay to love and protect her with his very life? Almost deliberately he laid a hand on Fingala's arm, his eyes half closed though he watched the man like a cat, and saw the tightening of the muscles on the strong cheek-bones. Yes, Sir Kenneth was a jealous man, and that jealousy could be born out of love for Fingala. Or desire? Sir Andrew did not know. All he knew was that she was a very desirable woman and Sir Kenneth was no doubt a lusty fellow. He wanted love for his angel-lady, and not merely desire.

They were all being seated round the huge table in the great hall, and the maidservants carried in platters of steaming hen broth and good vegetables grown in the plots of land around Rathay. There was elegance in this old castle, thought Sir Andrew, more elegance than he had been allowed to believe in the tales he had heard which had come out of Scotland.

But times had changed in recent years. King James was generous with his earls and barons who supported him, and many more merchants and traders were bringing their fine-quality goods into the country so that the nobles were enjoying a more gracious form of living. The table was well appointed with beautiful silver and goblets which Sir Andrew would have found joy in possessing. The ladies dressed well, and beautifully, and were well used to making decisions without reference to their lords. That helped the household to run more smoothly, and added to the comfort of the castle.

In fact, now that his wound was healing and his body stronger, he was enjoying his stay in Scotland, thought Sir Andrew. Soon he would have to leave Rathay and ride to Kilblain where the Earl Seton had arranged for a visit to Edinburgh, in order that he could look upon this young nobleman, Richard of York, at close quarters.

'There is little time to lose,' Sir Kenneth was explaining. 'Already the king gathers his army together, and the nobles support him, even if they mislike his cause. I ride for Edinburgh with my men within the week. How say you, sir?' He turned to Sir Andrew. 'Two more days only, I would say, then if you are to see this man before he rides with King James at the head of an army to invade England, and challenges King Henry to the throne, you must be well enough to ride by then. Will you be ready, or is it a lost cause?'

'He is still too weak,' said Fingala.

'He must not risk his life again,' Judith also protested, her eyes wide with anxiety.

'Then it is a lost cause,' said Kenneth, rather heavily.

'I have told you, I will be ready in two days,' said Sir Andrew. 'We may have to ride at a slow pace, but every step of the way will bring us nearer to journey's end. If I can rest at Earl Seton's place for a day, then we will be in Edinburgh within the week.'

'That was well said,' said Patrick approvingly.

Sir Andrew smiled briefly, but his eyes went to Fingala. He had promised her that he would carry out the duties for which he had been hired, and his eyes told her that he would make the supreme effort for her sake. Colour tinged her cheeks and her eyes grew soft.

'It is better a lost cause than you injure yourself further, Sir Andrew,' she said.

'Not so. It is important to thee, Lady Fingala. Many men have laid down their lives for a lady, and I would count myself fortunate for a lady such as thee. But I only risk discomfort.'

'And pain!'

'I am certain that our English nobleman will not consider his personal discomfort in this matter,' said Sir Kenneth, rather loudly.

He had been watching closely the looks which had passed between Fingala and Sir Andrew Heron, and he had no liking for what he saw. Many men fell in love with women who nursed them back to health, and this man was as susceptible as any he had met. He had agreed to wait for Fingala in marriage, but now he began to believe that he had made a great mistake in that agreement. He should have sent for the priest, and sealed the bargain, whatever she said, or however much she protested. He could have kept an eye on Rathay, as well as Cardowan, and thereby kept faith with Sir James Montgomery.

And now Patrick had returned home, but only for as long as it would take to gather his men together, then they would both have to ride behind their king into England. And for such a cause!

'Would you wish me to call the maidservant and ask for fresh meat, Sir Kenneth?'

He came out of his thoughts, startled, as the soft voice of Mistress Judith Heron spoke in his ear. She had a sweet voice, low and musical, and her accent was strange but attractive to his ear. He turned to look at her, noting the softness of her rounded cheeks and the light in her eyes. He had been informed by his squire, who passed on all gossip from Rathay into his willing ears, that Fingala had sought to rouse Patrick Montgomery's interest in the girl, but he found her too young for his liking.

Kenneth moved easily in his seat and noted the emerging womanhood in her young body. No, the maid had left childhood behind, and she was not averse to being attracted by a man. No doubt Patrick had put her off with his glowering looks, but she was doing little to hide her admiration for himself. It would be a passing fancy, of course. Very young females often fancied themselves in love with an older man until they were settled into a suitable marriage.

'It is a kind thought, mistress,' he said, softly, 'but I do not ask for more meat. This is sufficient for my needs, and more. The dogs can eat what I leave.'

'There is honey pudding, sir — a favourite of the Lady Fingala's. Perhaps that is more to thy liking.'

'Perhaps that is so. I have a very sweet tooth and I admire all sweet things.' He allowed his eyes to rest on her soft lips.

Judith blushed and looked away, well aware that her father's eyes were upon her. She should be behaving with quiet decorum and had been at fault in addressing herself to Sir Kenneth Buchanan, but he was the most attractive man she had ever met. She had never seen a man more tall and strong. He had the air of a man who had seen and done great things with his life.

But he was going to marry the Lady Fingala, Judith reminded herself, and now her eyes were downcast. He was one of this country's greater noblemen, and she had been a forward young woman in making conversation with him at all. Her father would not be pleased with her.

'Is not the honey pudding to your liking, ma'am?' he was asking, and this time his eyes were full of laughter. She was a pretty child and too good for Patrick Montgomery in his opinion. Patrick was a fool where women were concerned. How could he set his sights on Catherine Gordon and say that he would have no other! Where was the man's eyes that he could not see this child was a prize worth having, always supposing he could encourage the girl to make such a sacrifice for him? She deserved better than a stupid husband!

'I think I have eaten sufficiently, sir,' she was saying, quietly.

'I am sorry that your appetite is so poor, mistress. Perhaps we all need something to stir the blood.'

'Stir the blood, sir?' Her eyes were wide as she turned to look at him.

'That is what I say. Perhaps Sir Patrick and the Lady Fingala would consider holding a night of revelry with dancing and music before we all ride out once again. The days of mourning the death of Sir James are now over. What say you, Fingala?

Shall we arrange a feast for tomorrow? The men shall go hawking and we will excuse Sir Andrew.'

'I crave some gentle exercises before I ride for Kilblain,' Sir Andrew put in.

'That you shall have. You can sit a quiet beast and take part as you will. What say you, Fingala? And you, Patrick?'

'It is fine sport,' Patrick agreed, and his eyes twinkled a little as he looked at Judith, 'and we do have a quiet beast.'

'It is fine sport,' said Fingala, 'and we will be happy to provide the feast, but I am not happy that Sir Andrew should go hawking, even on a quiet mount.'

'You are like an old woman attending to a chick, I declare,' said Kenneth, his eyes glinting dangerously. 'Women have a fondness for keeping men helpless when Nature would have them about their business once more.'

'I am aware of my obligations, lady,'

said Sir Andrew, gently. 'I will only do what my strength allows. I thank you for your concern.'

She looked at him, and he no longer tried to hide the love in his eyes for her. Fingala's heart shook. She knew that she had liking and respect from Sir Andrew Heron, but — but love? She was betrothed to Sir Kenneth. She loved Kenneth.

But — did she? Fingala felt confused. She was beginning to doubt her own feelings. These two men, so very different, pulled at the different aspects of her own character, always at war with one another. She admired the gentleness and courtesy in Andrew Heron, yet the strength and arrogance of Kenneth also called to her heart. But she only had one choice. She belonged to Sir Kenneth Buchanan, as though the knot had already been tied.

'We will have a feast-day then,' she agreed. 'Tomorrow. I will arrange it. You can help, if you will, Judith.'

'That I will, and gladly,' said Judith,

with shining eyes.

Patrick turned to look at her, and his eyes sharpened. Something had caught the girl's imagination. She was more animated than she had been since the first day she rode into Rathay. Until now he had thought her a dull child, though sometimes roused to impertinence and laughter at his expense. Now she was smiling with true happiness, and there was radiance in her face. It suited her, thought Patrick. She was a prettier child than he had believed.

9

The feast of Rathay was a celebration which Mistress Judith Heron would never forget. It made her life at Havarden seem a dull affair and she no longer pined to return home with her father. The music and dancing called to her youth and high spirits, and she sometimes felt that with the encouragement of the Lady Fingala, who had clothed her in dark red velvet, a sprite had leapt into her heart and was guiding her footsteps as she stood up with Sir Kenneth and sometimes Sir Patrick, ready to dance every dance.

All day the maidservants had been alternately hectored and cajoled into cleaning the great hall and setting aside the carpets which now replaced the rushes. The floors would be left bare for the revelry. The tables were laden with pies, honey-cakes, fruit tarts, joints of roasted meats and fowls, and hot spiced wines which were heady if one drank more than enough.

Sir Andrew was content to watch the revelry, though he noted that Patrick had arranged for the castle to be guarded at all times, and for the guard to be changed frequently. He had a sense of foreboding that this night would end a chapter in his affairs. The Lady Fingala's dainty feet had twinkled as merrily as anyone's in the dance, but soon she came over to sit beside him and to bring two goblets of wine for refreshment.

'Your jollity will be heard over half the countryside,' he remarked. 'Surely it is a beacon, lighting up Rathay?'

'It is so,' she agreed, 'but we are at peace with our neighbours. We do not fear attacks at this time.'

'Yet there is the sound of marching men. I can feel the tramp of their feet vibrating the air I breathe. It is ever an ominous sound.'

'Aye, they march. Patrick is gathering

our own men after the revelry. A messenger has arrived and you are all on the march in the morning. None would dare to attack us this night since we are too well guarded. There are great rumours afoot that the young Duke of York has already been identified as a Flemish gentleman called Perkin Warbeck. But the King will not believe the accusers. If you can say that he is not Richard, Patrick also wishes to be an accuser, and I do not like it, Sir Andrew. The king has great energy and enthusiasm when he takes up a cause. He will not like to be thwarted. It depresses him, and once again he is aware of the punishing girdle he wears in memory of his father. He blames himself for his father's death, and gives himself great bodily discomfort. Sometimes — ' she looked at him, then beyond him — 'sometimes I feel that the pain of his body will distort the judgement of his mind, and our king will make an unwise decision one day which will bring great trouble upon himself, and upon our country.'

'I trust it will not cast its shadow upon you, lady,' said Sir Andrew. 'Is it true that you marry very soon with Sir Kenneth? My daughter appears to be charmed by his dexterity in the dance.'

'It is true,' she agreed. 'I promised my father that I would see Rathay in the care of a good mistress before I go to Sir Kenneth. But my mother is now a great deal stronger than she was after my father died, largely thanks to your daughter who has entertained her and brightened her mind. She has prevented my mother from turning in upon herself, and has put her back to normal living. Also Patrick will very soon choose a wife. He must see now that Lady Catherine Gordon — or perhaps it is Catherine of York — is surely lost to him, and he will be sensible about finding a good wife. I will go to Sir Kenneth as soon as he returns from this campaign. The nobles are not hot for blood, and it should be ended soon.'

'I would have thee happy, Lady Fingala. You have my undying gratitude and — and love.' He stared at her squarely, and she coloured vividly.

'The love of a dear friend, I hope, sir,' she said, breathlessly.

'Not so. The love of a man for a woman. Why should I lie to you? I am now in my right mind and almost my right bodily strength. I want you to know that I bear thee a great love, and if you wish to call upon me at any time I am ready to lay down my life.'

'I — I should not listen,' said Fingala. 'You confuse me, sir. All my life I have known that my destiny lay with Cardowan.'

'I wonder if we all follow our destinies,' Sir Andrew mused. 'Who would have believed that I should find love in an old Scottish castle?'

'Please speak no more,' she pleaded. 'I cannot listen to such talk.'

Suddenly the large gong which Fingala kept in the great hall and used to summon John Cuthbert, should she need him urgently, resounded loudly and the revellers grew quiet and looked towards the end of the hall where Sir Kenneth Buchanan stood, tall and powerful, but brightly flushed from drinking his wine. Beside him stood a dark-robed figure who cringed a little and stepped back towards the shadows.

'Nobles and friends,' Sir Kenneth roared, 'we are gathered here in order to take pleasure in our revelry, and now I ask thee to take more pleasure in witnessing the fulfilment of a contract of marriage between the House of Buchanan and the House of Montgomery. The Lady Fingala has been my promised bride for six years. She did not wish to leave Rathay until Sir Patrick Montgomery returned to take up his inheritance. Well, Sir Patrick is within the gates and his mother, the Lady Agnes, is mistress of the castle. The Lady Fingala is now free to go to Cardowan. We will be wed through yonder chamber in the chapel of Rathay before I go to fight by the side of our king for a cause dear to his heart. I have brought the priest — here, fellow, show us thine authority to perform the marriage — and it is very fitting that our friends witness the joining of hands between the Lady Fingala and myself.'

With a few strides and many shouts of well-wishing and encouragement, he came to take Fingala's powerless fingers in his own and to lead her towards the chapel. How could he arrange a marriage in this way without consulting her? She wondered, furiously. Yet how could she argue against fulfilling the contract in front of their many guests? She looked up into Kenneth's face, seeing that behind the jollity there was a look of cold, deadly determination.

The priest had been hustled along to stand before them. He was a shy, elderly man who took the chapel service every Sunday at Rathay. He would have preferred to be at his prayers rather than mingling with men and women abandoned to such gaiety. But he had known for some time that the marriage contract was due to be fulfilled. He was here for such a purpose, and he must carry it out as demanded by the young lord.

Holding out his arms, he began to recite the words of the marriage ceremony even as Sir Kenneth took Fingala's hand and they stood in front of the priest. Almost in a daze she found herself murmuring her responses at a nudge from Sir Kenneth. His fingers felt like steel as they held her own.

Then it was over and the priest declared them wed before God. Sir Kenneth kissed her lips, then turned his bride to face the assembled crowd, so that Fingala found herself face to face with Sir Andrew Heron, and her heart leapt then weighed heavily in her breast. His eyes were dulled with pain when he saw that she was lost to him, and it seemed that he turned away from her, and out of her life.

But she could never have belonged to Sir Andrew, thought Fingala, even as she accepted congratulations and many cheers and toasting in wine from her own people, then their many friends and the nobles present. She felt that she was living a dream in which her contract had been honoured to Kenneth Buchanan and her future settled without realisation of what had happened. It was all much too sudden. For the first time in her life Fingala felt too confused to think clearly.

Kenneth had pulled her into his arms and began to lead the dancing once more, claiming that it was his right to do so with his new bride.

'Where are thy smiles, lady,' he asked. 'Is not this a night for making merry? We are husband and wife at last.'

'I like not thy methods, *Husband*,' said Fingala in a low voice which trembled with anger. 'How dare you put me in such a position? You gave me no choice but to obey you, but I would have preferred to plan my own wedding which would be very different from this hole-and-corner affair in the midst of our revelry.'

'You have already had your chance, lady,' he said, and his own voice was like ice. 'There is much *I* do not like, but my wishes were not consulted. Now I have made my own plans. I am no longer willing to be treated like some oaf, or weakling, awaiting thy pleasure, lady. It is done, and a good night's work. Come, smile, my sweet bride. Enjoy thyself. Tomorrow we ride to battle. Thy luck might be good and Fortune might find thee a widow ere too long.'

She shivered violently. 'Do not say so, or I will think the Devil is in thee.'

'For this night, it could be true. There is anger in me which is still not appeased.'

★ ★ ★

Patrick's restless eyes swept the crowd, then he caught sight of Judith Heron. Her face was very white and her eyes seemed to be fixed on Sir Kenneth Buchanan as though she had been mesmerised.

'She mislikes the marriage,' Patrick murmured to himself. 'Stupid child. She shows her misery for all to see and read. Her face is like to an open book. Yet why should she be miserable? She has only recently met Sir Kenneth, yet her eyes follow him everywhere as though her love had been given to him and would serve no other.'

Patrick bit his lip with annoyance. What was there about Kenneth Buchanan which roused such feelings in the hearts of young women? Judith was ready to follow Sir Kenneth to the death, yet she had shown all too clearly that she did not enjoy his own company. Patrick felt piqued. He had done a great deal more for her than had Kenneth Buchanan, yet she despised and insulted him.

Deliberately he made his way towards her.

'Will you stand up with me, Mistress Heron?' he asked, formally.

'I — I regret, sir, that I am tired,' she said, hastily, unable to meet his eyes in case he saw the tears which swam in her own. 'The revelry is more than I am used to. I ask leave to retire, Sir Patrick.'

He was silent, staring down at her fixedly.

'And I ask thee to stand up. Your fatigue is easily put behind you if you learn to enjoy the revels. A child would be fatigued, I grant you, but I understand you are now a young female, and no longer a child. For a lady in the full vigour of her youth, I would expect you to dance until the piper falls asleep.'

'I have told you, sir, that I am unused to such revelry. I ask leave to retire.'

'And I ask thee to stand up with me. Your fatigue is easily put behind you, if you learn to enjoy the revels. A child would be fatigued, as I say, so let us have proof of this new grown-up young female.'

Judith stared at him miserably. 'You laugh at me, sir.'

'No, I but ask you to stand up with me.'

She did so, and danced with all the verve required of her, but the light had gone from her eyes and the radiance from her face.

When the dance ended, once again she begged leave to retire, and Sir Patrick nodded his dismissal without speaking another word.

Judith's heart felt empty. If only she were the Lady Fingala, how much she would want to be the bride of Sir Kenneth Buchanan. But he was not for her, and Judith was too young to weather such disappointment and to put a brave face on it.

She threw herself down on her bed and gave way to a storm of tears.

10

On the following morning the castle of Rathay swarmed with men and maidservants, each of them busy about their affairs. The Maid of Rathay — no longer a maid — was not in the best of tempers and hectored the serving maids into preparing good food, simple but nourishing, for the departing soldiers, also provisions for a long march. The castle must also be brought into good order after the revelries of the previous night, and many tempers were as sour as the stomachs after the drinking and feasting.

Sir Andrew Heron, now that the Lady Fingala Buchanan was irrevocably lost to him, treated her with dignified courtesy, and all the deference due to a hostess to whom he owed a great deal.

'Sir Andrew will ride to Edinburgh

where we assemble before marching south,' Patrick decided, 'because Seton will be there with his men. The king plans to call up support for Richard of York in Northumberland. Having set eyes on this Richard, Sir Andrew is then free to return to England under a small escort once again. It will be safer to travel to the west, since the armies will be marching to the east.'

'And Mistress Judith?' asked Fingala of her brother.

'It is best that she remains at Rathay until her father returns for her,' Patrick said, firmly. 'The eyes of serving men might well be turned towards her, if she ventures out with her father.'

In truth the maid was growing into a comely woman, as Fingala had said, and it might be well for him to offer for her and to try to coax her into marriage. It was said that the Lady Catherine, now wife to Richard, was growing to love her husband and was giving him full and open support. It was common talk that she was whole-heartedly in favour of the man. That had angered Patrick. He had known Lady Catherine well, and it had not mattered to her that he was ready to lay down his life on her behalf. Now she was ready to accept such bounty, but to take it on behalf of her husband, and Patrick demurred at this state of affairs. The Lady Catherine was still as beautiful as ever, and people referred to her as the white Rose of Scotland, but in his heart Patrick knew that his dream was now over, and that it had only been a boy's dream. Judith was in the right of it. He had acted the boy instead of the man.

Now he should look to the House of Rathay, especially since Buchanan forced Fingala's hand and married her before she could draw breath to protest. Not that she would wish to do so, thought Patrick, though she did not like having her decisions made for her. But he admired Buchanan for the way he could handle Fingala. It took a strong man to stand up to his sister.

Patrick stroked his chin. He should also marry now and try to find a young woman who would be mistress of his castle, and bear his children to perpetuate his family. Mistress Judith might be no bad choice, and Fingala had no longer pushed and prodded him to marry the girl. He liked to make his own decision. But now Fingala could not wait for Sir Andrew and his daughter to be gone from Rathay. Patrick had scratched his head and wondered if Fingala were not becoming jealous of Mistress Judith's transparent admiration for Sir Kenneth. Surely, now that the knot was tied, she need have no further fears of this nature. She was in a strange mood, this strange sister of his, thought Patrick, and she was running through Rathay like a flame, and no one dared to question her instructions.

'We cannot take the maid with us,' Patrick told her. 'It is too dangerous. Men are on the march to Edinburgh, but I will see that Sir Andrew returns via a different route. I am more alert to guarding our safety than Squire Keith. Seton should never have sent him for Sir Andrew.'

'I will have no peace until they are returned to their own home,' said Fingala, her cheeks now warm with colour. 'I want them to leave Rathay.'

'The maid must remain here,' Patrick insisted. 'I have pondered the matter, Fingala, and perhaps it would be no bad thing if I considered her for marriage.'

'She is too young, just as her father is too old!'

'Too old for what?' asked Patrick, staring. His sister spoke senseless words at times. 'He is young enough for most affairs, and his eyes are certainly sharp. He can look at this Richard, and tell us if he is the boy he knew.'

Fingala said nothing, though her soul seemed to churn inside her body. How had it happened that she had allowed Kenneth Buchanan to bind her to him under the sacred marriage vows? One night in the marriage-bed had been enough for her. He was a rough man, made rougher by drink, and he had used her ill and had not respected her as a gentlewoman.

She had accused him of finding his pleasures with maidservants and forgetting that she was a well-born lady, and he lay on his bed and laughed until the bed shook. Then his breathing had evened, and he snored loudly until morning.

Fingala had no stomach for facing the day, and irrationally all her pent-up anger and frustration had been directed against Sir Andrew. *He* would not have used her so ill, ignoring her cries of pain and protest on their wedding-night. *He* would have been gentle with her, and would have taken her in love.

But he was also weak, she decided with anger. When Sir Kenneth had tossed the priest in front of them, he had not stepped forward to stop the marriage even though her eyes had pleaded with him. His had only reflected his own misery and disappointment. If he had been a bold man who truly loved her instead of himself, he should have claimed her as his own, and even fought Sir Kenneth for her favours. That is how she would have conducted the affair had she been a man. But beyond his look of anguish which still pained her heart when she thought about it, he had done nothing. He was not worthy of her, and she did not want to be constantly reminded of him by having his daughter remain at Rathay as Patrick's bride. She had made a mistake in that matter. The quicker Sir Andrew and Mistress Judith Heron were back to Havarden again, the better.

* * *

Mistress Judith was suffering the severe pangs of first love which had gone sadly wrong, and when she knew that she was not being allowed to ride out with her father from Rathay she could not hide her disappointment, though she accepted the decision with dignity, where she would once have stormed and wept. Now it was easy to see the need for her to remain here until her father returned.

Patrick would have been happy to seek an opportunity to speak with her on her own, and to say goodbye to her, but she preferred to retire and sit with Lady Agnes Montgomery, and merely acknowledge his presence with a dignified incline of her head when he came to take leave of his mother.

'Fingala will stay at Rathay until we return,' he promised, 'since Mistress Judith is under her protection. She will not go to Cardowan until Sir Kenneth can take her there as his bride. It is the best way.'

'She has honoured her contract,' Lady Agnes said, with satisfaction. 'Kenneth sought my advice on the matter before the night of revelry, and I was pleased to give my consent, Fingala would have found excuses otherwise, and sacrificed her own life to Rathay. It is better this way.' She smiled at her son and held out her hand. 'She has honoured her contract and kept her promise to her father, but it is for you now, my son, to honour your House.'

Patrick glanced at Judith.

'Perhaps the matter will be settled soon, Mother.'

'I know you are a dutiful son and a worthy master of Rathay. God be with you, Patrick. It is time that men no longer fought one another in battle, though that is the way of our world since the beginning of Time, and no doubt will ever be so. Go with God.'

Patrick bent to kiss her cheek, then turned to Judith.

'Go with God, sir,' she repeated, but her voice was politely formal.

★ ★ ★

Fingala's farewell of her new husband took longer and was inclined to be quarrelsome. Sir Kenneth claimed to have been in his cups in the marriage-bed, and would fain have dallied longer with his new bride now that the fumes of his wine had left his head clearer.

'You *were* in your cups, sir,' she assured him, 'and you took little heed of my feelings in the matter. You were rough with me, and a bully.'

'Women like a manly lover,' he said, pulling her into his arms. 'Would I be more to your liking as a mamby-pamby fellow like the Englishman who is full of the courtesies and all the niceties?'

'He is no weakling!' she said, hotly. 'He has been sore wounded, yet he pulls himself out of his sick-bed to save you and our other nobles from fighting battles which are unnecessary, and not honourable.'

'He has smooth manners,' said Kenneth, lazily.

'He is a gentleman.'

'Aye, and if I had not married you in

such a fashion he would have plucked my bride from me as that bride might pluck a flower. I am no simpleton, Fingala, so do not think I could not see what was pushed under my nose. I had to take thee, or he would have slid thee from my arms with his smooth talk and gentle words. I know very well what he was about, and I could see the tentacles already reaching out to touch your heart.'

'You did not have to drink too much ale in order to do so. You hurt me, Kenneth Buchanan.'

'Oh, you will mend,' he said, shrugging. 'You are not a milk-sop, Lady Buchanan. You would not do for Cardowan if you were a poor thing. I will conduct you to your new home before I go to Edinburgh. My mother is waiting to receive thee.'

'It is best that I stay here until — until you return,' she objected. 'Have you forgotten my promise to my father?'

'I have forgotten nothing. It is your

brother who forgets. Why cannot he find himself a wife? He is not uncomely and has all his teeth, and his limbs. The English child might do. The king finds favour for those who marry English women. He would have us turn our country into a — a simpering, posturing, laughing-stock like — '

'That is not true,' she cried. 'He only desires us to cultivate a little more grace and elegance. As to Mistress Judith, you should have married her yourself. She sees no one but the great Sir Kenneth, ever since you rode into Rathay. The child pines for thy favours.'

He grinned and tilted up her chin to look deep into her eyes.

'That is what I like to hear, my sweet bride, a little jealousy. You are jealous of Mistress Judith. You are my love in spite of all your vapours and protests. Come now, order your maidservant to guard the door and we will be a-bed again. This time we will have time to be soft and gentle with each other, and you will hear loving words whispered into your ear. I swear that you will not be ill-pleased with the man you have married. I promise you pleasure in my arms, sweet one.'

'There is no time,' she cried. 'There is much to be done, arranging for supplies for your march, and a thousand tasks which require to be supervised.'

'Patrick will take care of all of them, and as to supervising the maidservants, they all have heavy heads after last evening. They will go at their own pace.

'My own head is equally heavy. They will also have sour tempers, and I vow that my own good temper could change quite quickly if you do not meet me in love,' vowed Sir Kenneth. 'There is no time for argument.'

She swallowed. She had not enjoyed her wedding-night and had no wish for a repetition of the experience, but even as she hesitated Sir Kenneth called loudly to one of the maidservants.

'We would be alone, your lady and

I,' he told her. 'Guard the door.'

She blushed and giggled as she bobbed a curtsey, then took up her position with her back to the door. Fingala had no choice but to obey, and to allow her new husband to act the maid as he undid laces and removed her gowns and petticoats, even as he unbuckled his own heavy garments.

Pressing her lips together, Fingala crawled into bed, then her husband was beside her, taking her in his arms. This time he was gentle and loving, speaking tender words or admiration of her beauty and her good spirits as a woman. This time her heart stirred a little.

'You see — ' he said, softly, as he stroked back her beautiful golden hair and laid a roughened finger on her fine white delicate skin — 'you see, you are woman after all, Fingala. Some say you are a witch. Well, maybe you have bewitched me because I would have torn this castle apart to find thee if any more time had been lost in gaining thee for my bride. Had there been no contract between us, I would have made one. Can Sir Andrew Heron say the same? Would he have fought for thee? Would he be ready to die for thee? I am ready to kill any man who looks at thee, and cut down any man who would ever harm thee. And I am ready to die for thee, Lady of Cardowan.'

She looked into his eyes and saw laughter in their depth, and something stirred in her, but she decided that it was anger at the way he considered his own feelings above hers. Everything must be as *he* wished.

'You do not yet understand,' he said, gently, raising himself on one elbow to look at her. 'You do not yet see.'

'See what?'

He sighed. 'I will have to teach thee another lesson after I have returned from serving the king. Meantime, ponder on me and what I do for thee, my sweet bride, but I expect to see love in thine eyes for me when I return home.'

'And I may remain here at Rathay?'

His eyes seemed to bore into her own.

'It is as I say. Ponder on it.'

He nodded as he rose from their bed.

'Aye, you may stay here at Rathay. I will know where to find thee, if I leave thee here. Always it is Rathay, Rathay. My mother and father grow old, Fingala. Soon Cardowan, too, will need a good mistress. My mother is frail but she has made her peace with God, and has blessed me in case — ' he grew a trifle hoarse — ' in case she is not in this world when I return. I — I may never see her again.'

'I did not know, Kenneth,' she said, her eyes troubled.

'Why should you? Is your interest ever stirred by Cardowan? Do you care what happens to my House? I have taken thee as my wife, and hope that there will be a child of our union.

If I do not return quickly, look to that child, Fingala. That child will belong to Cardowan, not to Rathay.'

She said nothing, and he caught her arm.

'Do you swear?'

She stared at him. So his loving moments on their marriage-bed had been merely his way of begetting his child on her. He was anxious for an heir for Cardowan.

'There is no need to make me swear, Kenneth,' she said, tonelessly. 'I know my duty.'

'I do not want your duty,' he said, and the smile had gone from his eyes. 'I want your love and loyalty. I do not want to see your smiles as you languish for the Englishman. If you persist, I would not be so very gentle, Fingala.'

She looked at him, and he saw something in her eyes which made him pause. He caught her hands and looked into her face, keeping none of his feelings back.

'You have my loyalty,' she whispered.

'And thy love?'

There was a commotion in the passage, and the maidservant's voice could be heard, also Sir Patrick's. Kenneth raised his hands to her shoulders, shaking her.

'And thy love!' he insisted.

'Aye,' she gasped.

'You promise?'

'I promise.'

He swung away from her and walked out of the bedchamber, buckling his heavy coat, and she sat back down on the bed. Once before she had made a promise. What would her promises be worth if Patrick did not bring home a bride? Kenneth would never allow her to stay at Rathay.

She smoothed down her clothing which had been crumpled as it was tossed on to the floor, and fastened the laces with trembling fingers, then she hurried out of the bedchamber and for the next hour or two she was too busy for more thought.

Finally, the men, strong and brave,

rode out of Rathay so that Fingala's tears wet her cheeks. She had bidden farewell to Sir Andrew who bowed before her formally, then she had embraced her brother. Then Sir Kenneth stood before her, and she received a formal kiss from him on her forehead.

'We, Sir Andrew and I, may return within a short time,' Patrick told her, 'after which I will join Sir Kenneth and our men. We will ride together, since he is now my brother and my own kin.'

'I will look out for you,' she promised, 'as will John Cuthbert.'

'Do not worry, I shall keep an eye out for Sir Kenneth, as a brother would.'

She nodded and wanted to weep like a child. Her heart was sore, but she hardly knew why. Was it because Sir Andrew was going out of her life? But he was returning fairly soon once his mission was accomplished. Then Sir Kenneth? She saw his eyes glittering as they stared back at her after his leave-taking, then he walked towards her again.

'I cannot force thee to love me,' he said, in a low voice. 'I know this is so. I cannot force such promises from thee, Fingala. We will forget that it has been made.'

She did not reply, hardly knowing what to say. Then he was gone and there was nothing more for her to say.

Suddenly she was aware of a slight figure at her side, and turning, she saw Judith standing beside her.

'I hate to hear men riding out,' she said. 'I grow afraid that I am looking upon their faces for the last time. It has rarely happened at Havarden, but I expect you are used to it, Lady Buchanan.'

Fingala's heart shook, then suddenly she wanted to call Kenneth back again. Suddenly she wanted to see love in his eyes for her once more.

She felt lost, and bereft, she who had never before felt incompetent at dealing with problems which came up whilst her menfolk were away. And always her father and brother had allowed her to take responsibility for such things on to her own shoulders, and she had not felt lost and helpless when they rode out.

But Kenneth wanted to shield her from that. He was a man, and he wanted her to feel protected and loved by a man. That was what he had meant when he said she had not understood.

Would that suit her nature? wondered Fingala. Would she enjoy having a man to make decisions for her? She sighed deeply. She had become confused by these two men, her husband whom she had known for so long, and the quiet English gentleman who had treated her with courtesy. Her heart felt empty and torn, but she did not know for whom she yearned. She was no longer so sure of her own wants and needs.

The men had gone. The ground had vibrated to the sound of the hooves of many horses and riders, and there were many men also on the march. Times were troubled again. Soon they would be grumbling about their cause when their garments were soaked by the rain and blew against their bodies in the strong wind. They would complain when their bellies were empty and the ale had been replaced by water.

'God keep them,' she muttered.

'Amen,' said the girl.

Fingala turned away and went down to the emptiness of the great hall.

11

Fingala had never felt more tired and lethargic. With the departure of Sir Patrick, once again the running of Rathay fell upon her shoulders, even though Lady Agnes offered her help wherever it was needed.

Fewer men had been left to help with the running of the estate, and plots still required to be dug so that their fruits could be harvested and the people could be fed. Complaints were many, and quarrels between the wives and farmers and farm labourers were more fierce than those which broke out between the men. The women would arrive at the castle, bleeding and torn like cats, their voices shrill in their denunciation of one another and ready to scratch and tear in their rage.

At one time Fingala had not understood their disputes and had made quick decision which had settled the matter, mainly because of her own anger and impatience. Those decisions had not tackled the root-cause of such disputes, but the contestants were more afraid of The Maid than they were of one another. Now she began to see that many quarrels were born of fear and insecurity, and she tended to question further and ponder the matter a little more so that her decisions were more pertinent, even if they presented difficulties.

Judith had sidled into the great hall one day when Fingala was holding court, and gradually her interest was caught so that she listened carefully to the problems of the people who lived on the estate, and to Fingala's assessment of them, and her advice as to the settlement. The right to certain acres of land was disputed, also water and the access to water by animals of one farm through the land of another.

Fingala pored over maps and documents, trying to make decision which were fair, but even as she took longer in her assessment so her tiredness grew and her temper shortened. Soon Judith was being given her share of responsibility, but she did not protest. Her respect for the Lady Fingala was growing daily, even as she began to love Rathay. As every part of the estate became more familiar to her, and the people began to accept her as the young guest at the castle, Judith found it beautiful, and wandered within the precincts after she had undertaken the duties of the day.

'I am sorry that it is necessary for me to call upon your labours,' Fingala said one day when the petitions were no longer so numerous. 'Now that the men have gone, the women must take charge, and as you will have learned there are a great many tasks which require attention.'

'I like the tasks,' Judith told her. 'Only by taking responsibility for some of the work do I see the beauty and — and even grandeur of Rathay. I am glad that Sir Patrick forced me to remain here when my father rode out. Sometimes — sometimes I see how much I have lacked sense in the past and how childish it is to insist upon having my own way.'

Fingala looked at her thoughtfully. 'Truly you are growing into a young lady of sense,' she said.

Judith coloured at the praise. 'I will go and help Lady Agnes with mending the linen. She enjoys talking and I enjoy listening to her.'

Fingala's nose wrinkled. 'The needle is a sad weapon in my fingers. When I go to Cardowan, I intend to find a sewing maid who will stitch for me.'

★ ★ ★

News was brought to them a few days later that the king, accompanied by Richard of York, was on the march to Northumberland, but little was known about Patrick and Sir Andrew Heron, though the messenger who rode in was very sure that Sir Kenneth Buchanan was riding with the king.

'I saw him leave with his men, my lady,' the man said, wearily, having spent two days in the saddle. 'Sir Kenneth has joined the king's forces and they ride through Berwick.'

'You see what this means,' said Fingala, turning to Judith, even as she ordered rest and refreshment for the messenger.

'What can it mean, my lady?'

'That Richard is truly Duke of York. Your father, Sir Andrew, must have identified the man as being the claimant to the English throne, otherwise Earl Seton would have presented his evidence to the king, and there would have been no need to go to battle. The man would have been conducted out of Scotland, no doubt with scant ceremony, and our men would be riding home.'

Judith paled. 'Then it means war with England,' she said. 'King James is supporting Richard and will fight our

King Henry to give Richard his rightful place on the throne. That is how it will be, will it not, my lady?'

Fingala looked at the girl rather sadly. She could see the deep anxiety on her face.

'That is how it will be.'

'And the Scottish nobles — Sir Kenneth and — and the others — might not look kindly on — on the English.'

'If you mean that you are likely to be made prisoner if our countries go to war, I do not think so. Your father was brought into our country as a guest, and he will be conducted home with due courtesy.'

Judith's eyes were downcast. 'I — I do not like being the enemy of — of Sir Kenneth,' she said, 'or — or Sir Patrick,' she added, belatedly.

Fingala eyed her levelly. 'Sir Kenneth and I were betrothed for many years,' she said, quietly, 'and now we are married, and the ceremony performed in the chapel with the blessing of our priest. I think you admire him, Mistress

Judith. I speak plainly because you are a sensible woman and will not waste too many hours in dreams. It is too late now for changes in our lives. You had better understand that if your heart has been touched, it should be allowed to heal, then given to another. I carry Sir Kenneth's child within me, and my future is now decided, and is by the side of Sir Kenneth at Cardowan. I am his wife, and the mother of his child, and that cannot be undone.'

Judith's face had lost all colour, then the blood rushed to her cheeks, and tears started in her eyes. Fingala had laid a hand on her arm.

'I had to speak plainly to you,' she said, quietly. 'I cannot see thee yearn for something which is beyond our power to give.'

Judith pulled herself free, then rose to her feet, and Fingala expected her to rush from the room and make her way to her own chamber. The girl lowered her head and stood very still for a while, then she turned to face Fingala.

Her eyes were very bright, but she held herself well in control.

'I do not understand why you should speak so to me,' she said, almost defiantly. 'I admire Sir Kenneth Buchanan, even as I admire many noblemen who — who are strong and brave — as my father was, at one time, though now he prefers to live like a scholar. I am happy that your marriage is so well blessed, lady. It is what I would wish for you and — and Sir Kenneth. As soon as my father returns I shall be more than happy to ride with him to Havarden. That is my home. It has been an — an experience for me to come here with my father, but I hope that it will be over soon. I think it is time we both returned to the world which we know.'

Fingala's eyes were bright with admiration. The girl had great courage and dignity, and she had never admired Mistress Judith more.

'Well said,' she approved, 'and perhaps you have the right of it. It may not be entirely a secret that — that I admired your father, Sir Andrew, even as you admired my husband. He is a fine man and I am sure that my life has been enriched through knowing him, and listening to his philosophy of life. I, too, will be sorry to lose the companionship of such as he, but it is better this way.'

Some of the taut lines on Judith's face relaxed and there was pain in her eyes as she came to sit beside Fingala.

'I thought it was so,' she confessed. 'It is not easy, being a woman, Lady Fingala.'

'No, it is not easy,' said Fingala, gently.

Judith left her to go and find Lady Agnes, and Fingala looked after her thoughtfully, her eyes shadowed with fears which she dared not express to Judith. If Sir Andrew's mission had now been accomplished successfully, he should surely by now have reached the outer boundaries of Rathay, and be riding in at any time. But the messenger who had brought news could tell her nothing about Earl Seton, Sir Patrick Montgomery or Sir Andrew Heron.

'It was said that the king's mood was not of the best,' the messenger had told her. 'He has been grieving once again for his father, and blaming himself for the circumstances of his death. Another year has gone by and he has added weight to his belt of repentance.'

Fingala nodded with understanding and sympathy for her king. James had accompanied those Scottish noblemen who rebelled against his father, James III, on to the field of battle at Sauchieburn and could not now excuse his youth as a contributory factor towards his own conduct at the time. He had been, in his own eyes, an accessory to the death of his father and he deeply repented the sin of such a crime. He wore an iron belt next to his person, and every year he added to its weight, and in so doing he also added depression to his spirit.

Fingala sighed. Everyone in the kingdom knew of how the king suffered because of this dark corner of his life. He needed a wife, she thought, a good woman who would make him laugh a little and rouse him out of such depths. He needed a wife, even as Patrick needed a wife. But she could see, now, that Mistress Judith was not the woman to make Patrick happy. She had been wrong to try to throw them into each other's arms.

But she dared not search her heart too deeply about Sir Andrew Heron. She only knew that every day brought great emptiness to her, and she could not understand her own feelings. She only knew that she had changed. She had told Mistress Judith that she carried Sir Kenneth's child, but she was, as yet, unsure as to whether or not this was strictly true. Her signs were late, but her body's cycle was often in such case, and she could not rely on such a guide. She would have to wait a little before she was sure. But she felt that a shock might be needed to cure Mistress Judith of her useless dreams over Kenneth, and she was hopeful that she had been correct. The girl had fought her battles, but she would return to her old life with more heart.

★ ★ ★

The days seemed to pass endlessly, and although Judith questioned Fingala closely as to when her father might return, soon she no longer broached the subject, and she grew well aware of the apprehension in Lady Fingala which she tried to suppress under a hive of industry. The castle must be made clean. The stores must be counted, and fresh supplies ordered, or harvested from the estate. The horses must be groomed and made ready in case more horses were required by Sir Patrick, even the old creatures which were useless for battle.

Then one morning a messenger rode into Rathay, and when John Cuthbert came to tell her of his imminent arrival, Fingala's heart leapt and she made ready to receive him. Now, at last, she would have news of her brother, and Sir Andrew Heron. But most of all, she might have news of her husband.

The messenger was squire to Earl Buchanan of Cardowan. His wife, Margaret, Countess of Cardowan, had that day died of her fevers, and Earl Buchanan desired that his new daughter-in-law should travel to Cardowan and take up residence as mistress of the household.

12

'What shall I do?' Fingala asked herself for the hundredth time.

If she left Rathay for Cardowan, it could be many months before she saw Rathay again, but if she ignored Cardowan's request to fulfil her duties as wife to the heir she would be failing in her promises to her husband. Ought her husband to be considered before her dead father? To whom did she owe most loyalty? Was her mother capable of running Rathay by herself?

The questions tumbled over in her tired mind, but the answer appeared to be plain. She owed her greatest loyalty to her husband. Already she had carried out the duties imposed upon her by her father for many months, and surely no more could be asked of her. But if she left for Cardowan at this moment she would never see

Sir Andrew Heron again.

And that would be no bad thing, her common sense told her. Sir Andrew should mean nothing to her now that she was married, yet she had a great longing to see him, if only for a short time. Sighing, Fingala went to find her mother and to explain the position to her.

Over the past few weeks the Lady Agnes' health had improved. She was now reconciled to the death of her husband, and she was beginning to take up the threads of her life again within the castle. She spent long hours in the chapel, praying for the soul of her husband and the safety of her son, but she was also practical enough to keep the linen mended and to supervise the maids who tended the sleeping quarters.

Occasionally she ate her food in her room, but for the most part she joined everyone else in the great hall, taking her rightful place at the table. Her complexion was a better colour now that Judith had encouraged her to walk with her within the boundaries of the castle, and the fresh air had done much to restore her to good health.

'Cardowan has sent for me,' Fingala told her, deciding that a direct approach was best where her mother was concerned. 'I think it is best that I should leave Rathay and take my place as wife to the heir of Cardowan. I think I carry his child within me. It is best that the child be born at Cardowan.'

Lady Agnes' faded eyes brightened. 'That is good news, my daughter,' she said. 'It pleases me that your seed has quickened. I will miss you, but Cardowan is not so very far away. Your father thought that was an advantage when he arranged the match. You can bring the babe to Rathay when it is born, and I shall hold my grandchild in my arms before I follow thy father to the grave. I hope you have many more fine sons and daughters who will grow up into fine men and woman. My own babies lie with their father.

My children were born weak, except for you and Patrick.'

'Do not talk so much about the grave, Mother,' Fingala objected, shivering. 'If I go, I shall have to ask thee to hold the castle until Patrick returns. Now he *must* marry. He must find a wife. He knows very well that Lady Catherine is lost to him, and if, as it seems, that the Duke of York *has* returned from the dead, which must please his aunt, Margaret Beaufort, then the Lady Catherine is now a Duchess and higher than any in the land. If King James scores a success with supporting Richard, then she will even be Queen of England. Our poor Patrick cannot do so much for her.'

'She should have been content with Rathay,' said Lady Agnes.

'She had no choice. The king arranged her marriage.'

Lady Agnes sighed deeply. 'I can hold the castle, Fingala,' she said. 'The servants respect my authority, and I shall find ways of showing that

I am still a strong woman — in will, if not in body — and they will not dare to disobey me.'

'They will not dare,' Fingala echoed, 'because I will give John Cuthbert the power to deal with any recalcitrants, and if there be trouble he will send a messenger to Cardowan and the matter will be dealt with from there. Mistress Judith will help thee until Patrick returns. She will be a companion and she has surprising sense for one so young.'

'She is a good child,' Lady Agnes nodded. 'We will manage very well between us.'

* * *

There was still no news of Sir Kenneth, nor yet of Patrick and Andrew Heron. Fingala thought that she ought to join her mother in prayers for their safety in the small dark chapel where their priest came to hear confessions, then she bade her maidservant guard the door of her chamber where she made her own prayers. She had her own communion with the Spirit of God. It might not have been approved by the priest, but she only knew that her body felt alive with strange powers after she had opened her soul to the great Holy Spirit, and that from the depths of her soul she received a communion with God which gave her strength to face all things.

The maidservant who guarded the door had whispered that she had seen strange golden light coming from the chamber of the Maid of Rathay at such times, and that a draught had blown down the stone corridors when the air outside was as still as the grave. But the servants liked to tell tales during the long dark evenings of winter, and often they lost nothing in the telling.

Fingala packed her bags, but before she could ride out John Cuthbert came to find her and to tell her that Patrick was riding in, and that the English lord rode by his side.

'Thank God,' Fingala whispered. 'Thank the spirits who listen to my prayers and who answer those prayers within the great powers of the earth, and the heavens.'

She had learned, over the years, not to ask for miracles, and if her prayers could not be granted she always made supplication for the strength of will to suffer adversity. Now she waited, with all that strength, for any news which Patrick might bring.

They rode into the castle looking weary and travel-stained, but Fingala had already ordered the servants to be ready to receive them with whatever was necessary for the comfort of the men. Food was prepared, water boiled and fires lit in their quarters where they would rest.

'I am happy to see thee, Patrick,' Fingala said, thankfully, after her brother had walked into the great hall and threw himself down on a long settle. Sir Andrew accompanied him, his face lined with weariness and his eyes suddenly older.

'Aye, our journey has been more hazardous that I would have thought. When men are on the march the blood-lust is up for some of them, even though for other, such as ourselves, the cause is not great enough to stir us to anger. But the Armstrongs were ready to do battle, and when they got word that we escorted an English nobleman we had to dunt a few heads and have our own knocked about in return. But we have accomplished our mission, though for what I do not know.'

'What happened?' asked Fingala eagerly, as she poured out mulled wine into goblets to refresh the men.

'Later,' said Patrick. 'We are all weary and sick of the saddle. We must rest and our men and horses must be fed, not to say ourselves because my stomach grumbles with emptiness. The Armstrongs did not succeed in beheading our guest, but they took his meat and mine.'

Judith would have rushed forward to question her father, but Fingala restrained her. She was avid for news, but the men were ready to collapse with exhaustion and hunger. Quickly she rapped out her orders, and included Judith in her instructions so that very soon the men were resting in clean garments, having supped a good nourishing broth before falling into a deep sleep which was almost a stupor.

'Their garments stink of blood,' said Fingala. 'There will have been a few gashes to bind up, I do not doubt. I will see that our men are being cared for properly and the wounds cleaned.'

Judith's eyes were wide with concern. 'I have never seen my father looking so — so wild and dishevelled,' said Judith. 'Why, he looks almost like a — a — '

'Scots nobleman,' Fingala supplied, smiling obliquely. 'Aye, our men tend to run at one another like fighting cocks whenever a cross word is spoken, though it is better now than it was in my father's time. Now they are beginning to tackle one another in the field of sport and in tournaments. The king enjoys such sport. There is more sense in that than in laying waste to one another's property, though men have been killed in tournaments when the games have become too fiercely fought.

'Sir Andrew will be himself when he wakes up, never fear. I — I expect you will desire to ride back to Havarden now. I hope it will be a reasonable journey for you both.'

'I must go with my father,' Judith agreed, and her eyes met Fingala's clearly. She was getting over her infatuation for Kenneth, thought Fingala.

Kenneth! Where was he? she wondered. She would question Patrick closely when next he woke up. She must know what had happened to him before she travelled to Cardowan.

'Life at Havarden was dull,' Judith

was saying. 'I did not know it, but my life was too quiet, and I would not care to go back to such quietness and — and stagnation. My father has his books, and his studies, also his writing of the law books. It is enough for him. I remember that my mother often sighed, however, for more pleasure and excitement. She was full of laughter and happiness when I was a small child, then she became quiet and had to spend her energies at the loom, or sewing fine tapestries. She said that she was growing too old to dance, but I think she longed to dance nevertheless. I enjoyed my dancing on — on the night that you were married, my lady. That was a merry night, full of music and enjoyment. I want to dance now and again when I go home, but there is no one to dance with me at Havarden. Young people do not call, only the older men who are also interested in the law. I will ask my father to — to try to arrange for me to serve at Court. It should be merry there also.'

Fingala regarded her thoughtfully. 'You do not wish to marry?'

Judith's eyes grew bleak, and Fingala saw that there was still desire in her heart for Kenneth Buchanan. She should feel jealous that another, very attractive woman admired her husband so much, but her own feelings were in such confusion that there was no room for jealousy in the tangle.

'I do not wish to marry yet,' said Judith. 'My father would find me a husband who is as quiet and gentle as himself. I do not wish to live such a dull life, and I would fain enjoy the pleasures of Court life for a year or two, then perhaps a marriage could be arranged for me. I would have my memories to keep my step light into old age.'

Fingala smiled and reached out to touch Judith's rounded cheek.

'Truly you have an old head on such young shoulders,' she said, 'and I am glad that old age is very far away for you. I have attended Court myself when my father was alive, and I admired the great barons and earls of our land, with their ladies. It was there we saw Lady Catherine Gordon, and Patrick lost his heart to her, so that maybe the fortunes of all of us have been changed. Now I must go to Cardowan, but I will find it hard to give up Rathay. I have great love for the home of my childhood, though I can also grow to love Cardowan's fair acres. It is richer than Rathay, but here I have already won respect and obedience. I must win it again at Cardowan.'

'That will be easy for you,' Judith assured her. 'It is natural to follow your lead, Lady Fingala. You have taught me a great deal since I have been a guest under thy roof. They are lessons I shall not forget.'

13

Fingala was impatient because Patrick was slow to answer her many questions when they all went to sup in the great hall that evening. She was leaving for Cardowan in the morning and had sent a messenger to inform Earl Buchanan, so that the gathering was bitter-sweet for her. She was happy to see her brother returned to Rathay and in good health, but sad that she would see so little of Rathay in the future.

She had avoided being alone with Sir Andrew Heron, making sure that Judith was by her side when she spoke with him. His eyes were troubled as they rested on her, and she knew that she still admired him, but their paths lay in different directions. All of her loyalty was now with her husband. And her love? Fingala avoided searching her heart. She did not know.

'Did you see the king, and Richard of York?' she demanded. 'I must know, Patrick. It is so like you to keep us in suspense!'

'We saw him,' Patrick nodded. 'We rode to Edinburgh where Earl Seton has a house, and Sir Andrew was made welcome and given sympathy because Earl Seton's men failed to give him proper protection on his journey north. But there was business to be done — but that is the affair of Seton and Heron.'

Sir Andrew nodded. 'He was very generous. We concluded the matter, whatever my findings.'

'Then we rode to where the king was gathering his army to march into Northumberland. We paid our respects, and Seton and I paid homage to James, then introduced our guest as Sir Andrew Heron of Havarden. Young Duke Richard did not recognise his old tutor, nor did he bear certain distinguishing marks of which Sir Andrew was more than familiar, having bent his gaze over the heads of the young princes many times. Ears cannot change shape, and it is well known that a tutor knows the shape of a boy's ear. We knew better than to denounce the man in front of the king, and thereby succeed in making James look foolish. Later, however, Seton craved audience, and asked the king to question Sir Andrew.'

Patrick bit his lip and his cheeks reddened angrily.

'We forgot to allow for the nature of our king. He is loyal to those he befriends. He would not believe that Sir Andrew could recognise Richard of York after all these years, and he would not see Sir Andrew to question him, or listen to his reasoning. Many have tried to show him that the fellow is an imposter, and some have curried favour with the king by assuring him that Richard is, indeed, the heir to the throne of England. The king prefers to believe *them*. So — '

Patrick was silent for a while.

'So?' prompted Fingala.

'So he has been informed of Sir Andrew's findings in the matter, but he has marched into Northumberland with the young Richard — nay, the young imposter — by his side. They say, openly, in Edinburgh that he is Flemish, and low-born, and coached by Margaret of Burgundy into believing that he is Richard. He *looks* like a prince. He has the *bearing* of a prince, and — and his wife is a great noble lady who — who loves him dearly. I no longer hope for her to be released from her marriage with him. I no longer desire a woman who has given her love to the king's protégé.'

There was a long silence whilst Fingala sighed, digesting the tale.

'And now?' she asked.

'Now I will see that Sir Andrew Seton and Mistress Judith have safe conduct to the English border, then I will join the king's forces in Northumberland. If the English people rally to Richard of York, then the king will continue to support him and — and I must support my king. If they do not, then it is my belief that the king will not continue to support Richard. He is loyal, but he is not so foolish. Richard has claimed that the people merely need a show of strength in order to remove Henry from the throne, and establish himself as King of England. If James finds this claim to be untrue — as Sir Andrew believes — then we shall be home ere the month is out.'

'That would be good news,' said Fingala. 'We are tired of fighting, tired of wars. It is time we all lived in peace, especially with England. It is time we learned certain aspects of good living from England even as they could learn from us. That would mean building up the quality of life, instead of destroying it.'

She was silent again, for a little while.

'Is Sir Kenneth riding with the king?' she asked.

Patrick's breath caught in his throat

so that he choked a little, then coughed.

'Aye — he — aye, it is maybe so, maybe so.'

'*Maybe* so!' said Fingala, sharply. 'What is this? Where is my husband? Has he decided that he does *not* ride with the king?'

'Oh no, indeed. You must know Kenneth Buchanan better than that. He is aye at the head of the king's soldiers. No — '

'Then what?' Slowly Fingala rose to her feet. 'You had better tell me, Patrick,' she said in a quiet voice.

'There was a skirmish,' said Patrick, unhappily, 'and we believe Kenneth was — was cut down, though there is no real news.'

Fingala looked at him, then her eyes widened and began to blaze.

'What are you telling me, Patrick. Are you saying that my husband has been killed? Have you waited all this time, knowing that tomorrow I go to Cardowan where the news is sure to be waiting, and have not *told* me what has happened?'

'We — we do not know for certain,' cried Patrick. 'I know that if I told thee, Fingala, there would be questions asked I cannot answer. We did not hear all the facts, and only the rumours were rife. A band of men tried to attack the king and Richard where they rested, and Kenneth Buchanan and Earl Cunningham were cut down defending the king. I know not if he is wounded — or — or worse — but I will find out. That I promise you. I had to make Sir Andrew safe, and see him over the Border, then I join the king.'

Sir Andrew had murmured confirmation that they had no real news, but Fingala was feeling as though a great searing flame was consuming her body. Now she knew that her feelings and senses had only been lying dormant. Now she knew where her true love lay, and that it lay with her husband, Kenneth Buchanan. He was a hard man, and rough, and sometimes he would treat her ill. But she, herself, was no milk-sop of a woman. She would not hesitate to strike a man down if he threatened the peace and well-being of her household, and she had no hesitation in calling upon the spirits of the universe to help her when she was troubled. She needed them now, but it seemed as though she was too late. It seemed that Kenneth, her love, was already dead.

She looked at Sir Andrew Heron who appeared to be old and tired. He was having to be protected, he and his daughter, before Patrick could go to Kenneth's aid, and even to find out news of what had happened. And his mission into Scotland appeared to have been unproductive in any case. Why had she been so attracted to him? He was a quiet man, immersed in his books as his daughter had said, but with humour in his gentleness which had been attractive. But his mild manners would never do for the Maid of Rathay.

'I would curse the man who has killed him!' cried Fingala, in a terrible voice.

Sir Andrew leaned forward and grabbed her arm.

'No, Maid of Rathay!' he cried. 'Do not curse any man. That curse may turn upon thine own head and thine own house. I can see love in your heart and eyes for Sir Kenneth, so ask God to protect him with love, and not with hatred and revenge. Are you not always saying that wars should be finished and that we should live at peace with our neighbours? Yet now you cry out when your own beloved is at risk. Only consider a little more deeply before you make decisions which you will regret some day.'

'My husband may be dead. My babe may not have a father.'

Sir Andrew's eyes darkened, but he still held Fingala's hand.

'Then give thanks to God that he still lives in thee.'

Fingala's shoulders began to shake,

but the sobs which shook her were dry
sobs. Only now did she realise how
strong her love had been for Kenneth
Buchanan. He had used her brutally,
but before he rode out he had taken
her in love, and that memory lived like
a flame in her heart.

'I love thee, Kenneth of Cardowan,'
she whispered. 'I will go to Cardowan
and I will make it a home worthy of
our son who will be heir to thy father. I
will go to Cardowan. That is my home
from now on.'

But she had withheld that love from
Kenneth before he rode out, so that
he had promised that he would not
force her love. If only she had not
been blinded — if only she had told
him of her love —

Patrick had come to hold her in
his arms.

'Do not grieve so, Sister,' he
whispered. 'None has yet seen him
lying dead. Only wounded. He has
been wounded before.'

But with the king's troops on the

march, Patrick felt cold inside that there *had* not been news of Sir Kenneth. If he were wounded, he must have been carried to a place of safety from whence word would soon have been brought to his wife. But no word had been received, and Patrick looked at his sister's suffering. She looked like a flame in her anger and distress. She would burn herself up if she did not remain calm.

14

Fingala and Patrick arranged that the castle be made as secure as possible before they rode out, and great preparations were made for them to leave after day-break the following morning. Patrick and his hench-men would accompany their guests to the English Border where his squire and a few well-chosen men would escort Sir Andrew Heron and his daughter to Havarden.

Meanwhile Patrick would ride, with his men, to join the king.

Fingala's heart was sore when she took leave of her mother. Lady Agnes' health was now much improved, but she was frail compared with the energetic, dominant châtelaine she had been in the time of Sir James. She had always looked slender and delicate, but her stamina had been great. Now Fingala looked at her anxiously and hoped she was equal to her task.

'John Cuthbert will send word to me if you need me,' she promised. 'I can be here in a day's ride. I will return as soon as I can after I have settled matters at Cardowan, but there will be much to do or the Earl would not have sent for me. Do you understand me well, Mother?'

'I understand you, Fingala,' her mother nodded. 'I shall watch for Patrick to ride home. He is now master of Rathay. It is his responsibility to care for the castle.'

'He will return very soon, I have no doubt,' said Fingala. 'It is a lost cause already, and I am full of anger that my lord has sacrificed himself to it. I pray that it *is* a lost cause, and that the imposter does not profit.'

'Hush, child, do not fill your heart with anger, not while the babe is yet to be born.'

'I only have anger in my heart,' said Fingala. 'It helps to make my lost love bearable. I did not do my duty by him. He should not have had to beg for my favours.'

A party of men had been sent from Cardowan to escort her to her new home, but Fingala took one or two of her own maidservants, willing to remain with her as companions for her in her new home, to join the party.

★ ★ ★

Cardowan lay to the north-east of Rathay and covered many acres of rich fertile land, so that the estate was rich and the Earl of Cardowan was one of the most powerful of the country's nobles.

Cardowan Castle had, however, been badly burned during the time of the present earl's father, and great care had gone into building the new castle, and incorporating many improvements in design and workmanship.

The staterooms were large and well proportioned, with rich hangings and beautiful floors. The windows were larger, and the façade well proportioned so that Fingala's eyes feasted on its beauty when Cardowan Castle finally came into view. She loved Rathay, but she could become very proud of Cardowan and felt an inner satisfaction that her son, if the child be a boy, would one day inherit these fair acres, and this magnificent home.

Inside the castle, however, she saw signs of hasty cleaning, no doubt brought about by her arrival, and the man who welcomed her, Thomas Murdoch, looked bleary-eyed and unkempt and bore the odour of strong spirits about his person.

Fingala's eyes hardened as they weighed up each other, and it was Thomas Murdoch who looked away. Rumour had been rife at Cardowan that the young Sir Kenneth had chosen a witch woman for a bride, and Thomas' heart quaked. She had all the beauty and purity of an angel, this new mistress, and that was always the mark of the devil!

'Where is Earl Buchanan?' Fingala asked, her voice as clear as crystal bells.

'He is a-bed, mistress,' said Thomas Murdoch. 'He has not been well since Countess Buchanan died, and Sir Kenneth rode out to join the king.'

Fingala's mouth was dry, but she stared at the man.

'What news of Sir Kenneth?' she asked. 'Has there been a messenger from the king?'

The man avoided her eyes. 'None, my lady, none as yet.'

'But there is rumour?'

He shuffled. 'Some say he has been wounded, my lady. One of our men returned, but only to look at his newborn babe, then he went back to fight with Cardowan. He — he said Sir Kenneth had been cut down, but no messenger has ridden in, my lady. The earl became ill when the news was brought to him.'

'By whom?'

'I — I felt it my duty to tell him what Jamie Ferguson had said, my lady.'

'I am glad that you set such store by duty, Thomas Murdoch. I will talk to you about your duty, and that of others, after I have spoken with the Earl,' said Fingala, and smiled.

The man quaked again. The new mistress shone like gold in the sunshine, yet she had ridden far and should be subdued with fatigue. He could fain have crept away from the castle, but he had nowhere to go. He had served the Buchanans since he was a boy, and his mother had sought shelter in the kitchens. Cardowan was his home. And this shining golden woman was his new mistress.

Thomas Murdoch grabbed a mug of strong ale and was about to drink it to warm the fears in his heart, then on second thoughts he put it aside. Some new instinct told him that he needed a clear head to deal with Lady Fingala Buchanan. Instead he went out into the courtyard and drew water from the well. The castle was new and fine, but the well was still old and water not as plentiful as it might be. But water splashed on the face and head was refreshing, and cool to his mouth, even though his stomach craved the ale.

The servants were milling around, asking about the new mistress, and in his desire for shock and drama, he told them. The new mistress was as beautiful as an angel, but she had driven fear into his heart.

Unaware of the impression she had given, Fingala was conducted to Earl Buchanan's chamber by a young maidservant, after she had shown Fingala her own rooms. For a moment she had caught her breath as she stood in the fine bedchamber she might have shared with Kenneth, but quickly she laid aside her travelling garments and placed a head-dress on her golden hair.

'I will refresh myself later,' she said, quietly, 'and for now I will pay my respects to the Earl of Cardowan.'

It was almost two years since Fingala had seen Earl Buchanan, and she was shocked by his failed appearance. His white hair was now scanty, and the flesh had fallen away for his florid cheeks.

'So you have come, Fingala,' he whispered. 'I would have honoured your wedding-feast, but my dear lady was in pain and had not long to live. We could not travel to see the marriage performed.'

Fingala coloured and bit her lip. It seemed strange to her now that Kenneth had been forced to resort to a surprise ceremony before she would consent to their marriage. Something had blinded her, and she had only seen Sir Andrew Heron at that time.

'It is no matter,' she said, taking his hand. 'I should have ridden to Cardowan before now, but the castle of Rathay has been unprotected.'

'Aye, we are ill served in Cardowan, with an old man and young women servants.'

'It is enough. I will see that everything is as it should be.'

He took her hand. 'They say — they say there is bad news of Kenneth.'

'I do not believe it,' she said, stoutly. 'I will not believe until we receive the king's official messenger. Sir Kenneth can take care of himself.'

'He is the last of our line,' the earl said, sadly.

'He is not the last,' said Fingala. 'His son will be born here at Cardowan, never fear.'

The earl's tired face began to fill with joy, and he pulled himself up in his bed.

'Is it so?' he asked. 'Are you with child, my daughter? Indeed, this is a great day for Cardowan. I was ready to die with sorrow for the ending of my house, but you — you have brought me new life, with the new life you carry. It is a great day.'

'Rest a while yet, sir,' Fingala said, gently. 'Rest a while, then I will help you to your feet. There is a great deal of life in you yet, and we need each other to restore Cardowan before Kenneth rides home.'

The earl stared at her, his eyes now as bright and sparkling as his son's.

'Do you think he will ride home?'

Fingala thought about the prayers and supplications she was about to make, and how she had already entrusted the care of her husband into the hands of God.

'If it be the Will of God,' she conceded.

She could only do a little by herself, but she believed strongly in the spirits who listened to her prayers.

'I must see that food is being prepared. I declare my stomach craves a bite.'

'It is poor fare. The supplies have gone with the men.'

'It will not be poor fare when I have attended to it, never fear. I will see thee fed with good broth, and thy linen made fresh.'

'Thy father was a fine man, and we

were aye good allies and never fought each other. I was happy to arrange the match between my son and thyself. It was a good day's work. I am happy with my daughter.'

'It was a good day's work,' Fingala echoed, then her eyes sobered as she thought again about Kenneth. He could *not* die! She needed him. She needed to tell him that she rejoiced in being his wife, and would bear his children proudly.

'Guard the door,' she commanded her maid-servant, and the girl turned pale. Lady Fingala was going to be no different at Cardowan from the way she had lived her life at Rathay.

★ ★ ★

Life at Cardowan took on a new pattern as the Lady Fingala took over the running of the castle. She had inspected every room of the castle and gathered the servants together and apportioned duties to all of them.

Thomas Murdoch had been given the choice of attending to his duties with more competence, and taking up residence in one of the cot-houses near the castle and growing his own food. He laid aside the strong spirits and cleaned up his person to Fingala's satisfaction. In truth he welcomed such guidance, and began to take a pride in Cardowan once more.

After a few days the earl rose from his bed, then took up his place in the business-room once more, and the word was spread round the tenants that the earl was again in full strength. There were some mutterings about the Lady Fingala, but none criticised her openly, and she was shown respect. She had chosen to ride a white horse, and declared she would wear white garments until Sir Kenneth returned. Her white figure became a familiar one round Cardowan, and when the farmers and cotters saw her genuine interest in their affairs they welcomed her eagerly and declared her a fine lady as she organised repairs to property and encouraged fair decisions in disputes. The castle became beautiful, and Fingala felt the babe beginning to stir in her womb and was content. She had not mistaken her pregnancy. The knowledge gave her an added beauty, as did her prayers for the life of Sir Kenneth.

15

The weather became wet and the winds
blew gently over the fair acres. Fingala's
heart stabbed with nostalgia for her old
home where the winds blowing in from
the sea were fierce and gusty, and the
raging seas battered ineffectually against
the rocks far below Rathay castle.

She went to look at the river which
wound amiably on three sides of
Cardowan castle, where the earl fished
for trout and salmon on his better days.
After heavy rain it could swell to a wild
torrent, bursting its banks and carrying
along broken branches and dead sheep.
The pounding waters soothed Fingala's
spirits and settled her mind, and the air,
clean and pure after the rain, brought
colour to her cheeks.

She was walking home when she
heard the sound of riders approaching
from the east, and for a moment her

heart quaked with fear. She was walking out without escort, having become used to peaceful living at Cardowan, but it was a foolish thing for her to do, as Thomas Murdoch had warned her, darkly. There were plenty of packmen and tinkers, not to mention bands of thieves, who would not give the Lady Fingala the same respect afforded by her own people.

Fingala measured the distance between herself and the castle, then looked around for a place of concealment, but the soft green fields had little protection. Minutes later the riders hove into view, and Fingala stared at them, then stared again. Soon she was running towards the horsemen where the leader had reined to a halt. She stumbled a little, panting for breath, and remembered the child she carried. But the man was hurrying towards her with great strides. Across his cheek was a great slashing wound, but Fingala did not care, and Kenneth's eyes were aglow with delight when he saw the look on his wife's face.

'Kenneth,' she whispered. 'I declare I must have spirited thee from the dead.'

'That you have, my dearest lady,' he told her. 'I was at the very door and invited to enter many times. Instead I decided I would look upon thy sweet face once more.'

'Oh, Kenneth!'

His great arms were around her, holding her close, and she did not care that his clothing stank of travel-stains and horseflesh.

'I had to see thee again,' she whispered, 'to tell thee that — that my heart is given to thee and that we will have a child soon.'

He looked into her eyes, then caught her to him again.

'I am the most blessed of men,' he said, in a low voice, 'I who love thee, Fingala, more than any other man can love a woman. But I return to thee scarred and hideous.'

'Not hideous!' she cried, staring at

him. 'The scar will heal. It has not marred thy looks. I am used to a scarred husband since it is not thy first wound.'

The jagged edges of the scar were still swollen and puckered, but Fingala had seen such scars before, and Kenneth would not be badly marked by his wound after she had treated it for him. She would soon heal it with her own ointments.

The roar of the river behind them was echoed by the rush of happiness to her heart, and it was only as they walked together towards Cardowan that she saw how tired he was and that his great strong frame had become enfeebled by loss of blood and fevers.

News had been brought to the earl who came out to greet his son as Kenneth and Fingala walked into the courtyard. The older man seemed to grow in stature as Kenneth walked forward to embrace his father, and his eyes were bright once again as he looked at Fingala.

'Now my happiness is very great,' he said. 'I can die in peace.'

'Die!' she echoed. 'Nay, my lord, there is to be no more talk of death. We are all young and can soon regain health and strength. You will live, sir, to see many grandchildren at Cardowan.'

His eyes twinkled. 'You married a witch, my son,' he said. 'It is what the servants say, but I say that she is a fairy child, and if she is witch, then she is a white witch, not black. She will bring glory to our House.'

★ ★ ★

It was after Kenneth had rested and he and his men refreshed with good sleep that Fingala began to hear the tale of the misfortunes of the king's campaign to restore Richard of York to the throne of England.

'Earl Seton had audience with the king and told him that Sir Andrew Heron confirmed the fellow an imposter, but James had already committed himself a great deal to the cause of the imposter and could not relinquish it so easily. We marched into Northumberland where Richard had claimed that the English people would flock to rally round him, but no one rallied, and James, having had time to ponder on Seton's words, began to look askance at Richard. I heard the young rogue begging James to save his people as we prepared to do battle, and the king replied that it was kind of him to beg for people who had no wish to acknowledge him.

'We were about to return to Scotland, after James informed Richard that he was about to abandon his cause, when we were set upon by a marauding party. I confess I was at fault and had not guarded myself, being intrigued by the affairs of the king and Richard. Being certain that the boy was an adventurer, I pondered on his origins and it served me ill. I was cut down before I could defend myself, and woke up in an English homestead with only two of my men to attend me, and the news that the army had returned to Scotland. The farmer and his wife had been well paid for our keep, but were ill-disposed towards us, and I was near to death many times as the fevers shook my body. But the wife gave me soothing drinks when her husband was in the fields, and I survived. My men were loyal and spent the waiting days helping on the farm so that they were softened to us, and I grew stronger.

'When I was well enough, I rode to Edinburgh, and the news is that King Henry has marched into Berwickshire with a raiding party in revenge for James' supporting of Richard, and has taken Ayton Castle.

'But James and he are not hot for a fight. The cause is too weak. The news in Edinburgh is that the adventurer is now in Cornwall, and that he is a low-born Flemish man who has been taken in hand by the Duchess of Burgundy, sister to King Edward IV, on order to give power to the House of York once more. James escorted the man to

Ayr, courteous to the last, and put him aboard a ship called *The Cuckoo!*'

'It is a stange tale,' said Fingala, her eyes shining as she listened. She knew that her prayers must have saved Kenneth from the very point of death, and she was uplifted accordingly. It seemed like a miracle that he was back at Cardowan, and that the fighting was over. There was peace in the land again.

'What of my brother?' she asked. 'Did you see Patrick? Have you heard if he joined the king after seeing the — the guests to the Border?'

'I did not see him,' Kenneth said, shaking his head. 'I was already wounded, and the fighting would be over, such as it was, before Patrick could join the king. If, as you say, he escorted the guests to the Border before riding to Northumberland, I would expect that he would return to Rathay when the king rode back to Edinburgh.'

'He had heard you were cut down.

I would not believe it.'

'Aye, there would be some who saw what happened, and I dare say I looked a dead man. But I can soon prove to my wife that I am very much alive.'

Fingala blushed. 'We will remember that I am with child, but there are many years ahead of us, and you will not find me unwilling.'

He pulled her into his arms.

'My white heart,' he said, 'they are years full of promise, and I vow I shall make thee a happy woman. We will find out if all is well at Rathay for your peace of mind, and I shall take care of the place if care is needed. I will send a messenger without delay.'

Fingala sighed and nodded as she rested in her husband's arms.

'I confess I am anxious for them, but it is right that you come first with me. I have a great love for thee, Kenneth,' she told him, shyly, and he folded her in his arms.

Epilogue

Where had the years gone? wondered Lady Fingala Buchanan, as she instructed her maidservants on which garments to pack before she and Sir Kenneth rode out for Edinburgh to attend the great celebrations for the marriage of King James to the Princess Margaret, daughter of Henry VII of England.

It was to be a wonderful occasion, thought Fingala, as Kenneth prepared to take part in many tournaments and sports of all kinds. The wound on his cheek was now only a fine-drawn line, and enhanced his already handsome looks.

Their two small sons, James and Alexander, were being cared for by nursemaids, and were in charge of their grandfather, Earl Buchanan, whose years were still sitting lightly on his shoulders. He had grown strong and vigorous again under Fingala's expert care. He doted on his grandchildren, and Fingala laughingly promised to bear a girl child, if she became pregnant again.

Several times she and Kenneth had ridden to Rathay where Lady Agnes was still mistress of the castle, and Patrick managed the estate. He had not married. It had been a satisfaction to him that the man who had taken Lady Catherine Gordon was finally proved to be the imposter, Perkin Warbeck. He had tried to invade England once again, through Cornwall, but had been taken prisoner and executed at Tyburn. His wife, Lady Catherine, had been brought to Henry VII, who had dealt kindly with her and had given her into the protection of his Queen.

But it took Patrick a long time to recover from the years he had spent in fruitless longing for Lady Catherine, even though his common sense told him that the Earl of Huntly, Lady

Catherine's father, might not have consented to the match. Rathay was not one of the greater estates. But Lady Catherine would have found Patrick a more honourable husband than a low-born Flemish man, he often argued. He had been cheated of his love, and after the war of 1497 he had returned to Rathay and rarely visited the Court. He would serve the king when bidden to do so, but otherwise he preferred to live quietly at Rathay.

But the marriage of King James to Princess Margaret of England had caught the imagination of the people, and everyone was excitedly preparing to go to Edinburgh for the festivities. Patrick was to ride with his sister and brother-in-law. They were invited to stay at the home of Earl Seton on the outskirts of Edinburgh.

Fingala tried on her court gown and Kenneth walked into her bedchamber as the sewing-maid finished stitching a small part of the hemline.

'How do I look?' she asked.

The gown was made of her favourite cream-coloured silks with an overmantle of apricot velvet. The head-dress was very fine, sweeping high from Fingala's forehead, and sewn with tiny pearls.

Kenneth stared at his wife, constantly enchanted by her beauty.

'I declare that the bride will not look more lovely,' he said.

She smiled. 'Shall I bear thy bugle-horn so that you can cross swords with another knight for my favours?'

He slapped her playfully. 'You forget that you are a gentle matron and not a young maiden. But I will be in tilts and tournaments, and may fight with some of the Border chiefs.'

'They are too fierce, even now,' said Fingala. 'They would kill one another, even though they know it is only for sport.'

'Not at this time,' Kenneth objected. 'We have a gentle lady to entertain and the Court is full of splendour.'

'I hope to find a wife for Patrick,' said Fingala. 'We will see that he comes out of his sulks with the king.'

'I will find him a wife,' Kenneth promised.

'A comely maid,' said Fingala. 'See that her teeth are well set. I would have Patrick happy, as we are ourselves.'

★ ★ ★

Patrick had trimmed his beard, and his court garments became him so that Fingala was proud of her menfolk as they rode into Edinburgh, where they joined with the crowds and cheered the king as he rode on his spirited horse towards Newbattle Abbey, where he was to meet his bride. How splendid he looked, thought Fingala, as he rode past wearing a jacket of crimson velvet bordered with cloth of gold. His lure, which he used for hawking, was hanging down his back, and his fine athletic body seemed to raise him above other men. Fingala's breath caught with pride. They could all be proud of their young king.

Fingala, accompanied by Sir Kenneth and Sir Patrick, rode behind the king to Newbattle, where the Earl of Surrey had escorted Princess Margaret and her attendants to meet the king, and there were loud cheers as the king leapt up in front of the princess as she rode her palfrey into the procession along the streets of Edinburgh.

The bride was very young and looked rather frightened, but as she caught Fingala's eye a warm smile passed between them, and the little princess relaxed. This was the most boisterous welcome she had ever received, and every now and again the procession was halted whilst great chiefs, in strange garb, would clash with one another, fighting fiercely until the king commanded them to cease.

Fingala and Kenneth became parted from Patrick in the crowds, then later they watched him distinguish himself at one of the tournaments staged that evening.

It was two days later when Patrick arrived at the house in Edinburgh where Fingala and Kenneth were staying, escorting a lady from the new queen's household.

'I have brought someone to renew acquaintance with thee, Fingala,' he said.

A moment later she was staring into a face which was at once strange, then very familiar.

'Mistress Heron!' she exclaimed, 'Judith Heron.'

'One of the queen's ladies,' Judith Heron laughed. 'I have been serving in the royal household since a few months after I returned to Havarden from Rathay.'

Fingala had almost lost her tongue. There were a thousand questions she wished to ask, but her eyes feasted on Mistress Judith, who had grown up into a woman of great beauty.

'You are still Mistress Heron?' she

asked. 'You did not marry?'

Judith glanced at Patrick, and shook her head.

'I found none to my liking, and I enjoyed serving the queen. Now I serve the Princess Margaret — Queen Margaret, as she is now. I was happy to return to Scotland.'

'And — and thy father, Sir Andrew?' asked Fingala. How strange to think she had once believed she might love Sir Andrew Heron. She admired him very much, but she knew her place in the world, and she had been born to live and die on Scottish soil, and to love the man who had married her.

'He is well,' said Judith. 'He has been writing books on the Law of England, and is ever researching his subject. He works quietly at Havarden, and the servants care for him.'

'I am glad,' said Fingala, simply.

It was like the ending of a chapter for her.

★ ★ ★

Before they left Edinburgh, Patrick brought Judith to see her and Kenneth once more.

'Mistress Heron has consented to marry me,' he said, proudly, and held Judith's hand.

Fingala stared at them, seeing the glances which were exchanged between them, and knowing that they had at last developed love for each other. Truly sometimes a plant took a number of years to flower, then to bear fruit, she thought.

'I come for thy blessing,' said Judith, shyly.

'You have our blessing, and gladly,' said Sir Kenneth, and Fingala kissed her new sister-to-be on the forehead.

'I told you that Patrick would make a fine husband,' she said, teasingly.

'This time I believe that is true,' Judith laughed, and Patrick threw an arm about her shoulders.

'We will find a priest after we have asked the consent of the king and queen,' he said. 'I want to return with a bride for Rathay.' He smiled at his sister. 'Sometimes those witch spells of yours take longer to work, but I am happy to have you say them over me.'

'Then you are happy, Patrick?' she asked.

'I am happy,' he said, simply.

Fingala felt the pressure of her husband's hand on her shoulder, and was content.

Other titles in the
Linford Romance Library

SAVAGE PARADISE
Sheila Belshaw

For four years, Diana Hamilton had dreamed of returning to Luangwa Valley in Zambia. Now she was back — and, after a close encounter with a rhino — was receiving a lecture from a tall, khaki-clad man on the dangers of going into the bush alone!

PAST BETRAYALS
Giulia Gray

As soon as Jon realized that Julia had fallen in love with him, he broke off their relationship and returned to work in the Middle East. When Jon's best friend, Danny, proposed a marriage of friendship, Julia accepted. Then Jon returned and Julia discovered her love for him remained unchanged.

PRETTY MAIDS ALL IN A ROW
Rose Meadows

The six beautiful daughters of George III of England dreamt of handsome princes coming to claim them, but the King always found some excuse to reject proposals of marriage. This is the story of what befell the Princesses as they began to seek lovers at their father's court, leaving behind rumours of secret marriages and illegitimate children.

THE GOLDEN GIRL
Paula Lindsay

Sarah had everything — wealth, social background, great beauty and magnetic charm. Her heart was ruled by love and compassion for the less fortunate in life. Yet, when one man's happiness was at stake, she failed him — and herself.

A DREAM OF HER OWN
Barbara Best

A stranger gently kisses Sarah Danbury at her Betrothal Ball. Little does she realise that she is to meet this mysterious man again in very different circumstances.

HOSTAGE OF LOVE
Nara Lake

From the moment pretty Emma Tregear, the only child of a Van Diemen's Land magnate, met Philip Despard, she was desperately in love. Unfortunately, handsome Philip was a convict on parole.

THE ROAD TO BENDOUR
Joyce Eaglestone

Mary Mackenzie had lived a sheltered life on the family farm in Scotland. When she took a job in the city she was soon in a romantic maze from which only she could find the way out.

NEW BEGINNINGS
Ann Jennings

On the plane to his new job in a hospital in Turkey, Felix asked Harriet to put their engagement on hold, as Philippe Krir, the Director of Bodrum hospital, refused to hire 'attached' people. But, without an engagement ring, what possible excuse did Harriet have for holding Philippe at bay?

THE CAPTAIN'S LADY
Rachelle Edwards

1820: When Lianne Vernon becomes governess at Elswick Manor, she finds her young pupil is given to strange imaginings and that her employer, Captain Gideon Lang, is the most enigmatic man she has ever encountered. Soon Lianne begins to fear for her pupil's safety.

THE VAUGHAN PRIDE
Margaret Miles

As the new owner of Southwood Manor, Laura Vaughan discovers that she's even more poverty stricken than before. She also finds that her neighbour, the handsome Marius Kerr, is a little too close for comfort.

HONEY-POT
Mira Stables

Lovely, well-born, well-dowered, Russet Ingram drew all men to her. Yet here she was, a prisoner of the one man immune to her graces — accused of frivolously tampering with his young ward's romance!

DREAM OF LOVE
Helen McCabe

When there is a break-in at the art gallery she runs, Jade can't believe that Corin Bossinney is a trickster, or that she'd fallen for the oldest trick in the book . . .

FOR LOVE OF OLIVER
Diney Delancey

When Oliver Scott buys her family home, Carly retains the stable block from which she runs her riding school. But she soon discovers Oliver is not an easy neighbour to have. Then Carly is presented with a new challenge, one she must face for love of Oliver.

THE SECRET OF MONKS' HOUSE
Rachelle Edwards

Soon after her arrival at Monks' House, Lilith had been told that it was haunted by a monk, and she had laughed. Of greater interest was their neighbour, the mysterious Fabian Delamaye. Was he truly as debauched as rumour told, and what was the truth about his wife's death?

THE SPANISH HOUSE
Nancy John

Lynn couldn't help falling in love with the arrogant Brett Sackville. But Brett refused to believe that she felt nothing for his half-brother, Rafael. Lynn knew that the cruel game Brett made her play to protect Rafael's heart could end only by breaking hers.

PROUD SURGEON
Lynne Collins

Calder Savage, the new Senior Surgical Officer at St. Antony's Hospital, had really lived up to his name, venting a savage irony on anyone who fell foul of him. But when he gave Staff Nurse Honor Portland a lift home, she was surprised to find what an interesting man he was.